THE MATTER OF SYLVIE

the matter of SYLVIE

A NOVEL BY LEE KVERN

BRINDLE & GLASS

Brindle & Glass Publishing Ltd.
www.brindleandglass.com

LIBRARY AND ARCHIVES CANADA CATALOGUING IN PUBLICATION
Kvern, Lee, 1957–
The matter of Sylvie : a novel / by Lee Kvern.

Print format: ISBN 978-1-897142-48-6
Electronic monograph in PDF format: ISBN 978-1-897142-89-9
Electronic monograph in HTML format: ISBN 978-1-897142-88-2

I. Title.

PS8621.V47M37 2010   C813'.6   C2010-903670-0

Editor: Lee Shedden
Design: Ruth Linka
Front cover image: Angel Strehlen
Author photo: Paul Rasporich

Canadian Heritage   Patrimoine canadien   BRITISH COLUMBIA ARTS COUNCIL   Canada Council for the Arts   Conseil des Arts du Canada

Brindle & Glass is pleased to acknowledge the financial support for its publishing program from the Government of Canada through the Canada Book Fund, Canada Council for the Arts, and the Province of British Columbia through the British Columbia Arts Council and the Book Publishing Tax Credit.

Mixed Sources
Cert no. SW-COC-001271
© 1996 FSC
FSC

The interior pages of this book have been printed on 100% post-consumer recycled paper, processed chlorine free, and printed with vegetable-based inks.

1 2 3 4 13 12 11 10

PRINTED IN CANADA

My J. My L. My S. for being

»»

Wednesday, July 1961 » Jacqueline, age 27

The sun shimmers on the horizon, a fierce red ball so impossibly large, sailor delight or the opposite, however the saying goes, so that Jacqueline Burrows knows this Wednesday is marked already at 7:00 AM. Her children run sideways across the neighbour's lawn in front of the row housing where she sits on the concrete step sipping cold coffee, and so later will the other wives and mothers whose husbands are also in the RCMP. The neighbourhood is a communal joke, like the joint holding cells for prisoners in the RCMP barracks in downtown Red Deer: these are the holding houses for the half-abandoned wives. Jacqueline glances down the street, but of course the other mothers and children aren't awake. No other mother's child rises with the first light and doesn't go to bed until well past dark like Sylvie does. The street is quiet with the exception of Lesa, five and a half, who blurs by on her red and silver bicycle with four-year-old Sylvie perched on the back, solid like a sailor in her element. Sylvie's scrawny arms are wrapped tightly around Lesa's sturdy waist, her black shiny hair swinging side to side in the sun. Nate, turning three next month, races after them but can't keep up.

"Wait," he hollers, and Lesa pedals harder.

Sylvie turns and grins her crooked smile back at him.

Jacqueline takes a drag off her cigarette that she buys by the carton at Farrow's Pharmacy three blocks over.

"Peter Jackson brand," she says to Mrs. Farrow, like ordering a man. Tall, slim, dark, a non-drinker, please. The long, cool fingers of her husband, the slim hips she had before the sweet, warm smother of children, the dark dark slip of nicotine in her lungs in the early morning; the non-drinker she is, her husband isn't.

She glances down at the pair of faded blue capris she's got on. The hole in the right knee that she'll have to patch when she has time, and her husband's RCMP sweatshirt that she puts on strictly for the scent of him, to remind her she has a husband. Constable Lloyd, her Dudley Do-Right from *The Rocky and Bullwinkle Show*. She smiles at their bedroom joke: does she need Dudley Do-Right's help? Dudley Do-Right will take care of that. Dudley to the rescue. Jacqueline's shiny Canadian Mountie in a pressed dark uniform. She misses him terribly some days.

Jacqueline exhales her cigarette smoke, folds Nate's cotton socks, Lesa's frilled blouses, Sylvie's plain T-shirts. Sylvie can't wear anything with decorative buttons or embroidered daisies or fancy doodads, otherwise she worries them with her fingers and her nails, also worried down to the quick, until the offending embellishments are mere holes in her shirts and elastic-waist pants. Jacqueline piles the clothes methodically into the broken wicker basket at her feet.

Sylvie and Nate flit by, running across the row of identical lawns in front of identical houses with Lesa in tow. Only no one else along the block has a daughter like her Sylvie. The other mothers are kind, yes, sympathetic even, but not one of them really knows what a day full of Sylvie entails. So beautiful, Jacqueline thinks. Sylvie, she means, despite the cruel jagged line across both lips and her slightly off-kilter eyes. Sylvie's face is alight, electric almost, where Jacqueline's is laden, weighted with effort. It's her eyes, Jacqueline decides, takes another drag off her Peter Jackson that tastes burnt; she notices she's down to the cotton filter. If you look at Sylvie's eyes, they are blackish-brown, bottomless really, but when Jacqueline looks at them those rare times when Sylvie isn't ripping through the house with Nate screaming after her or tearing around the neighbourhood with Lesa at her heels, it makes her want to cry.

It's as if Sylvie's wires are crossed and the only time she can find stillness in this fleeting, forever life is after a seizure, which she has three, four, five times in the course of a week. Then Sylvie lies perfectly still, eerily motionless as if already dead, her dark eyes dim, vacant. Jacqueline carries her into her bedroom where a single bed is pulled well away from the window—no toys or books or pile of misshapen stuffed animals, Barbie dolls, or mess of puzzles strewn across the carpet like in Lesa and Nate's room down the hall. She lays Sylvie carefully on the metal-frame bed and smoothes her hand across her forehead and cheeks until the colour comes back into Sylvie's thin face, her brown eyes come back into her head. There is something wholly tangible and wounded about brain damage—like a skinned knee beneath your pressed palm. Out of sight but never out of mind. How any god can plan such ruthless things for children is beyond Jacqueline.

God or no God, Jacqueline has love enough for all her children, although the love required for Sylvie is arduous and fervent, like Sylvie herself. Different than for Lesa, who is durable, responsible;

3

Jacqueline hardly ever worries over her. And then there is delicate Nate with his smooth child face looking up to her for guidance, approval, acceptance. His is another kind of love altogether. And it will be different again for the tiny embryo that Jacqueline knows by instinct (although she hasn't seen a doctor yet, or told Lloyd) is growing in her uterus at this moment. The sheer thought of three children under the age of six and a new one on the way makes her slump against the screen door.

Jacqueline turns sideways and catches her reflection in the living room window. She sees an indistinct, shapeless woman, not yet thirty years old. Where did *she* come from? Blackened circles beneath her eyes make the once startling violet of her irises that men used to glance at twice seem a dull grey. Her hair needs another henna or it's going to revert back to its original mouse brown. Her face, her hips are heavy with too much weight, too many children, not enough husband, she knows.

She sees Sylvie glide by the front steps; it strikes her how small, how light Sylvie's body really is for a four-year-old. Nothing but a kinetic moving mass of legs and limbs and summer-browned skin. How can it be then that Sylvie weighs so heavily on her mind?

Jacqueline finishes folding the laundry and looks up the street. Sylvie and Nate are both on the back of Lesa's tricycle now. Lesa struggles to push the pedals up the sidewalk to the steps. She doesn't stop until she reaches her mother's feet. Her face glistens with the effort. Jacqueline leans forward and spreads her arms. Nate and Lesa climb off the tricycle and stand a minute with their mother, but Sylvie sprints back down the sidewalk. Jacqueline brings the almost forgotten Peter Jackson to her lips, then remembers the burnt taste and flicks it off into the flowerbed on the side that is overgrown with three-leaf clover; she's studied it minutely day in, day out from her outpost on the concrete steps while her children campaign the quiet street in search of fun. No four-leaf clover to be found here. She gets up. Lesa beats her to it. Running, she catches Sylvie by the arm, swings her onto the neighbour's grass where the two girls pile on top of each other. When Sylvie gets up she is breathless and laughing. Jacqueline laughs too surprised in her tiredness, but how can she help it? Look at Sylvie, eyes dark, thrilling, her crooked mouth wide with her seal-bark laughter, her black hair shimmering in the brilliant light of early morning.

This is what Jacqueline will hold in her mind late tonight when she's past her limit and her Lloyd isn't home yet due to the nature of his job, due also to the fact that he can't look at Sylvie's skewed face, much less past it. There's reserve, remoteness in her husband that wasn't there before Sylvie came along that Jacqueline doesn't understand. Where is her Dudley to the rescue? Where is her Do-Right? The space between them feels limitless, without anchor, more than she can bear if she allows herself to think about it. She doesn't.

Jacqueline scoops Sylvie up in her freckled arms and buries her face in Sylvie's muscled belly; she has love enough for all of them, even her absent husband. What she doesn't notice is Lesa's face, sombre and intent, gazing up at her.

Wednesday, February 1973 » Lloyd, age 40

The street is empty save for the few pigeons that fly from the hardware–post office–general store to the roof of the hotel on Main Street. Corporal Lloyd Burrows stops his RCMP cruiser in the middle of the street, fishes a leftover El Producto cigar butt out of the ashtray, lights it with a wooden match, surveys the pigeons as they shuttle back and forth. Their dull grey bodies catching the sweep of yellow street light in mid-flight, then fading away, disappearing almost in the predawn—a child's game of *Red Rover, Red Rover, we call each other over*. Ice crystals hang in the still air and glitter like diminutive stars in the dark Wednesday morning.

The main street of Smoky Lake is also dark, and so is the hotel. Likely, Neville, the owner, hasn't come downstairs yet. Corporal Lloyd listens to the crackle of the radio, indistinguishable, just a sputter of noise and static, distant voices he can't make out, probably from the St. Paul detachment downriver. His own detachment is silent. His constables, at least the unmarried ones, are asleep in the barracks, his wife, Jacqueline, of nineteen years and children asleep in the attached house.

A quiet morning, quiet month for that matter, with the

6

exception of the eighteen-year-old boy—almost the same age as his daughter Lesa, who will graduate from high school next year—who threw himself into the frigid waters of the North Saskatchewan River last week. Yesterday his too-young, legal-age body turned up bloated and snagged on an ice floe on Corporal Lloyd's side of the river. Lloyd called Ed the ferryman.

"Ed?" Lloyd said.

"Corporal?"

"Yep, it's Lloyd. Listen, Constable Pete found our boy from last week and the poor kid's caught on our side of the river. Think you could tow it over to the other bank?"

Ed was silent a moment, in thought perhaps, weighing his answer.

"Godammit, Lloyd, you lazy son of a bitch," Ed said. "Make Constable Pete wade in and get *his* feet wet."

"There's a twenty-sixer in it, Ed. Your choice."

"How the hell am I going to do that?" Ed asked.

"Just do it when you only have one or two cars on board," Corporal Lloyd said and laughed like hell.

On the other end of the phone, Ed couldn't catch his breath from laughing.

"Let me know when you're done, Ed, and I'll call it into the St. Paul detachment myself and let them know they have a visitor," Corporal Lloyd said.

"Make it Jack Daniels," said Ed and hung up.

It's almost 6:00 AM. The light is on in the café adjacent to Neville's hotel. They should be open shortly. One more loop around the quiet town and Corporal Lloyd will come back and have a last cup of coffee before his graveyard shift is done at 9:00 AM. The price of a small-town detachment, a good corporal, he chooses to endure the midnight shifts the same as his constables. He sits in his cruiser, motor idling, glances down Main Street—his street, his town with a population of a thousand, largely Ukrainian with a Native reserve and Hutterite colony nearby, farmers, ranchers, one doctor, one vet, a school from K to 12, two gas stations, one drive-in theatre, one wife, three—no, four children if he counts Sylvie, but he seldom does. She's been gone so long that by rights, if out of sight out of mind means anything, Sylvie should barely graze his consciousness. But she does. The cruel imperfect line across her small lips, her dark eyes glimmering like Lloyd's, like the blonde's in the bar last night at Neville's—though the woman's were perfectly aligned, her deep russet eyes flashing at Lloyd, the all-Canadian Dudley Do-Right in uniform, who responded with a see-you-later nod, and he will see-her-later if the opportunity presents itself.

Yet Sylvie's there too; along with the decapitated mother from the head-on collision last fall, the mother's three-year-old child unscathed, wholly intact in the back seat of the car; the twenty-four-year-old male he found out in the middle of a farmer's field last year, summer 1972 in a 1972 Dodge on a ninety-eight degree Fahrenheit day—a breathless, sweltering day otherwise perfect for a parade. Occupant, deceased, wounds self-inflicted.

The countless lost futures, found fingers, wallets, limbs, stray shoes and families strewn across the highway. Blue babies in car seats, cribs, on doorsteps, the bitter backs of alleys, towns like his, reserves, cities—no one place or the other immune to the colour blue. And now the legal-age boy rootless and dead in the unforgiving North Saskatchewan River; the boy old enough to make decisions, young enough to know nothing of the Wonderful Wide World of Wickedness. He's seen that boy around town, he's sure of it, at the hockey rink, the drive-in: graduated from high school, shoulders squared up with the world, clean-faced, a bright, dazzling future. Surely the world his oyster, at his fingertips, innocent in his eighteen-year-old hands? Welcome to life and death, Lloyd thinks. He can chase the fairness all he wants, but he knows it'll never pan out.

Lloyd puffs on his cigar, gazes down the empty street. The north wind gusts, blows swirling snow, crystallized ice in the air, off the yellow street lights, the rooftops of Neville's hotel/café, the hardware store, Eve's Beauty Salon, down the dark soul-less sidewalks, the unpaved streets. Almost every lone moment he has, even now on this cold Wednesday morning, the dead and the living sit side by side like passengers in the back seat of his cruiser: Sylvie, like a live wire buried deep beneath the surface of his skin, the disquiet of an unfinished errand he can't bring himself to attend to. And all the others? Like blood that doesn't congeal.

Lloyd exhales the cigar smoke out the driver's window; the smoke hangs rigid, grey in the frigid white air. It's a disgrace, he thinks, a goddamned, cold-shouldered, undazzling disgrace, the imperfection of this world. He wipes his gloved hand across the dusty dashboard. When the sun comes up, he knows these night thoughts will dissipate. They always do, and in the few-lit hours of daylight, Lloyd will find reprieve in the salvo of a dark-lit lounge, strange women his elixir, his panacea, his magical cure.

He can already feel the perfect correction of Crown Royal in his mouth and the crimson lips of a blond stranger.

Wednesday, October 1987 » Lesa, age 31

Lesa Burrows shifts her fire-retardant cape squarely across her shoulders and watches as the plane dips down through the early morning Wednesday sky, through clouds that float like giant, murky-edged ships painted by Salvador Dali. The plane descends in time to catch the enormous sun cresting on the eastern horizon. It's akin to descending into heaven, but of course that's the opposite direction. The sun throws luminescent red-pink-gold light down over the green-black patchwork of the surrounding prairie where her mother lives. God-light, Lesa thinks, like those calendars you buy at Christian bookstores that show God's translucent-truculent hand reaching down from Heaven proper, radiant fingers of bullying light bestowing the Earth with His greatness.

The thought makes Lesa want to light up a John Player Special and blow smoke rings out the window into the Dali clouds. She digs through her purse for her silver M.C. Escher case with the birds and fish morphing into one another, pulls out a John, and tucks the cigarette into the top of her Superwoman boots for later. Although the boots aren't really super or anything special for that matter, just a pair of old fake-leather boots Lesa found in the dumpster a few years back when she was still a student at Emily Carr. Every time she puts them on she feels like young Maggie Trudeau about to go off and play polo with the Rolling Stones. Mostly the pleather boots collect dust behind the metal-fenced storage cage two floors below the apartment where she and her boyfriend, a sculptor/instructor at Emily Carr, live in Vancouver's West End. When she gets back home, she'll return them to the dumpster for public consumption.

She glances sideways at the other passengers drowsy in their business suits and somewhat dishevelled shirts, ties lapped loosely around their necks, ready to be knotted into action for their business meetings in downtown Calgary. At the moment, her sculptor boyfriend has a twenty-foot-high exhibition of burnt toast on Granville Island. The thought makes her smile, and a good-looking man in a blue suit in the next aisle smiles back. She tucks the highly flammable white wig that clings to her too-thin face behind her ears and looks out the window, senses his lingering glance. She wipes her sweaty palms on her legs. It's almost Halloween, or at least it will be in a few days. This year she's dressed as Storm from the X-Men for her dead father, for her younger brother, Nate, whom she knows will retrieve her from the airport. Their mother doesn't drive. Lesa knows it's too early for costumes, but that's the point, isn't it?

This is Lesa's first time back for the memorial dinner her mother puts on every October 31 since her father died three years ago. Her father with a rare kind of cancer that devoured him slowly over the course of eleven years—from the inside out like a ripening pear, then overtly so, and no one noticed until the dark bruises appeared on his yellowing skin.

Last year for Halloween Lesa dressed up in her father's RCMP red serge that she inherited and went around handing out Saran-Wrapped Spam (she was amazed to find you could still buy Spam) and cheese and lettuce sandwiches with a cigarette and spare change taped on top to the street people in her neighbourhood: an act of benevolence on behalf of herself and, unofficially, the RCMP. Where Nate and her mother choose grief, Lesa chooses a celebration of sorts.

She lifts her head, glances sideways at the blue-suited man. He's older than her sculptor boyfriend but fit, conditioned like an ex-hockey player, she imagines, beneath his expensive suit. His face is even, slightly tan, a few wrinkles around the eyes, nothing to be concerned about, the beginnings of age carved into his cheeks that Lesa finds attractive, wishes she had them herself. His hair is blond-to-grey. Late forties, early fifties? But it's his hands that Lesa is mesmerized by, oddly young. The man looks up and winks at a small, dark-skinned child playing peek-a-boo over the seat in front of him. He glances over at Lesa, who can't stop staring at his hands, his smooth boy-hands. She smiles at him, goes back to reading the instructions on the vomit bag in the pocket in front of her.

Lesa watches out her window as the plane slides down to meet the rushing grey asphalt and, beyond that, the city where her mother lives.

"Welcome to Calgary," the captain says in a voice that sounds like he just woke up.

"Currently, the temperature is minus eleven Celsius."

The passengers with ties knot them into action, take leather briefcases down from the overhead bins, pull on woollen coats. The man in the blue suit remains seated, waits as the mother ahead of him pries her child off the back of the seat, gathers her purse, a diaper bag, struggles with the overhead bin.

"Let me help," he says, standing to release the catch, then pulling down a pink and brown overnight case, which he offers to carry, but the woman protests in another language, Arabic perhaps. Then he withdraws his canvas duffle bag that looks like it could house skates and hockey gloves, pucks possibly. Lesa stands and smoothes her black rayon cape around her Spandex, then withdraws the cigarette from her super boots, wishes it were a joint instead, and waits to disembark. She hopes her Storm will be enough to get her through this Wednesday.

Wednesday, July 1961 » Jacqueline, age 27

It's 10:00 AM. The children have already had their lunch—Spam and cheese and lettuce sandwiches—although Sylvie has barely touched her sandwich but drained four glasses of watered-down Hawaiian Punch instead. Lesa runs back every now and then to take a bite of her sandwich, a sip of punch, and then she's off. Jacqueline sees that Nate has discarded his lettuce into the clover patch beside the front step that she means to rescue. She peers down and sees the faint purple-blue hue of strangled violets vying for room and light among the spreading weed. Like a disease, Jacqueline thinks, *dis*-ease, the opposite of ease, which is how everything feels these days. Today in particular. Perhaps it's the pregnancy, though she breezed through her others—except for Sylvie, with whom she had morning sickness from the start of her pregnancy through to the emergency high-forceps delivery because the umbilical cord was wrapped several times around her tiny neck. Jacqueline should have known that something wasn't right.

She leans down and pulls some of the clover out from around the shrinking violets and thinks about getting down on her hands and knees, but the *dis*-ease inside her is pervasive, like morphine coursing leisurely through her veins until it takes over her body entirely.

A pleasant enough feeling, but deep down, far beneath the surface, she senses the bottom. She knows she can't give in to the pull. She gets up and pours the remainder of her cold coffee onto the struggling violets. She glances down the street and counts one, two, three bobbing heads in the sunlight: Lesa, Sylvie, Nate. She goes inside the house to make more coffee.

She rose early this morning when she heard Sylvie stir in the room next to hers. The light outside, not yet dawn, was grey. She spread her hand across the double bed—Lloyd either gone earlier or not home from the night shift. She can hardly keep track anymore, the days and nights meld into a slow-motion blur. She tries her best to keep Sylvie occupied in the kitchen so she doesn't wake the other children. Lesa is a light sleeper and even the soft murmur of Sylvie's steady rambling is enough to rouse her.

Sylvie's dialogue is mostly directed at herself, the rare time at her mother or Lesa, when something, say, the striped orange kitten, Charles, that used to live next door and lurked beneath their front steps waiting to pounce on the children, appeared suddenly, playfully at Sylvie's bare, tanned feet. Sylvie yelped with surprise and delight. After Charles retreated and Sylvie could no longer find him, nor spot his glowing ochre eyes beneath the dark steps, she looked up, confused, puzzled. Unease seeping back onto Sylvie's fragile face, the familiar retreat beneath her dark eyes. But before that, the brief flicker of connection, the light on in Sylvie's eyes, that flickered also in Jacqueline's—with something other than the dull, protracted ache of an uncertain future.

That's all she wants—all any mother wants, Jacqueline thinks—is to keep her children close and warm and safe. And here was her

Sylvie alight and excited, in the moment—why she couldn't stop talking and peeking beneath the steps, gesturing with both her hands that looked as if they'd been put the wrong side up on her slender wrists. But then days, weeks, seven months after Charles the kitten disappeared for good, for *real* this time and no one knew where, well, Sylvie still refers to it as if it happened that morning.

Jacqueline has dreams of Sylvie—articulate, lucid, standing easily at the top of the basement stairs, as if the fall that Sylvie took down the wood stairs to the concrete floor last autumn, which caused her to retreat even further from the glissant surface of her eyes, had never happened. Or else she dreams Sylvie's in the middle of the living room floor, the sunlight slants through their picture window onto the turquoise carpet, radiant off the crown of Sylvie's pitch-perfect black hair. Sylvie peacefully sharing her Lego, something she never does, with Lesa and even Nate, who knows better than to fight with Sylvie over anything; she's small but has the strength of ten bears. And no one is fighting in Jacqueline's dream as she lounges on their tattered red and black tartan chesterfield watching *The Guiding Light* on the television in its entirety. Her Dudley Do-Right in the kitchen preparing Swiss steak for tonight's dinner.

Then Sylvie gets up from the Lego and comes over to the chesterfield. She tells Jacqueline that yes, she is trapped inside her body like Jacqueline suspects, and yes, her circuits aren't right, *that* she knows.

"But deep down," Sylvie says evenly, as if she's adult now. Sylvie puts her crooked face against her mother's freckled face so they see eye to eye like a Cyclops. "I'm here," Sylvie says, lightly tracing the darkened circles beneath her mother's violet eyes with her child

16

fingers. With Jacqueline's worst fear, her greatest joy confirmed, she looks into the bottomless pits of Sylvie's eyes. And here in her dream, always at the same point, is where Jacqueline opens her eyes to the black of her bedroom. She can't see a thing. Then Sylvie steps back from the waiting arms of her mother's dreams and returns to her private world.

Jacqueline pulls the sheet up, hugs her body until the shiver down her spine up her neck dissipates, then lies flat on her back, lets the tears run themselves dry before she gets up to check on Sylvie. The residue of dream like winter's breath lingers at the back of her mind, in the corners of her bedroom and Sylvie's, every room in the house, everything frosted over in white.

» » »

Now in the kitchen at 10:30 AM she fills the Pyrex with water, scoops an indeterminate amount of coffee into the metal filter, and puts the glass lid on. She lights the flame on the gas stove and leans down to also light her cigarette. When she rises, she sees a gaggle of kids sprint past the back alley. She looks for Lesa, finds her among the pack, with Nate bringing up the rear and Sylvie running as fast as her legs can go alongside but not in the pack. The other children don't know what to make of her.

"Lesa," Jacqueline yells through the screen window.

The pack stops.

"Mom?" Lesa says.

"You know you're not supposed to be in the back alley," Jacqueline says.

"Ok, Mom."

The pack takes off and rounds the corner to the front side of the street where the other mothers can see them. Jacqueline wanders back through the house. Toys are strewn across the carpet, the television is on, dancing bananas and apples—or tomatoes, she can't distinguish between them—polka across the dusty screen. If she could only get Sylvie to watch television, even for half an hour, she could rest. She's tired, although she suspects her weariness has nothing to do with the lack of sleep but with Sylvie, who can hardly sit long enough to eat, let alone stop and watch dancing fruit on the television. She looks at the broken wicker basket of laundry at her feet; at least the clothes are folded.

Wednesday, February 1973 » Lloyd, age 40

On his second loop around town, Corporal Lloyd turns the RCMP
cruiser a block west of Main, where the streets are rough gravel.
Lloyd pulls into the parking lot of the darkened Legion, sometimes
a gathering spot for the local teenagers, although not at 6:33 AM.
He sees a shadow in the entranceway and trains his bright lights
on the doorway. He gets out of his car. Christ, it's cold, minus
seventeen Fahrenheit with the north wind blasting all around. He
pulls his parka on and fishes his leather gloves out from the back
seat, leaves the motor running and his driver door open as he walks
across the lot.

"Jimmy?" he says.

The shadow doesn't move in the entranceway.

"It's all right, Jimmy. Come on out," Corporal Lloyd says.

Jimmy Widman lies prostrate on the snow-covered ground.
Lloyd goes over and bends down, peers into the man's upturned face.

"Jesus Christ, Jimmy. What the hell happened this time?"

Lloyd examines Jimmy's face in the cruiser's headlights. He takes
off a glove and puts his hand up to Jimmy's mouth. Jimmy's breath
is cold and shallow, reeks of Wild Turkey: his choice of bourbon

because it's reasonably priced and, taken straight up, gets the job done swiftly. Also, it reminds Jimmy of his father's farmland out east where undomesticated turkeys run feral. His father long since dead, his mother, too, by gunshot, Jimmy told Lloyd once when he was lucid, leaving Corporal Lloyd to work out the gritty details of that. No siblings that Lloyd has heard of. The wildness is all Jimmy Widman has left, Lloyd suspects. At least he's breathing. His nose is permanently mashed to one side. And he's missing a couple front teeth. No surprise there. He's the resident punching bag for every disgruntled male in the town. His lips are swollen twice their size and cut. His right eye is not visible anymore and there's dried blood, no, not dried, frozen blood pooled around his left ear. Lloyd looks at Jimmy's hands. They are flat and stone cold but smooth-skinned as usual, not a scrape on them—unprovoked, defenceless. Another unfinished errand that Lloyd must attend to.

"The Fleck brothers?" Lloyd asks.

Jimmy smiles up at the dark and blows foul air out of his mouth like smoke rings.

"Godammit, Jimmy. Stay away from those a-holes. They're going to kill you one of these times."

Jimmy tries to wink with his good eye, but his eye stays shut, a foretaste of the time when Lloyd knows he will find Jimmy not only stone drunk but also dead. Just a matter of time. His puts his finger on Jimmy's eyelid and lifts it. Jimmy's eyeball rolls around in its socket. Lloyd pulls the flimsy windbreaker around Jimmy. He retrieves a wool blanket from the trunk of the cruiser and rolls Jimmy onto it, then swaddles him like a newborn. He zips his own parka up against the wind. Thinks about his wife and children, his constables, the townspeople at home in their warm, safe beds. He knows he can't leave Jimmy here this time to sleep it off and eventually make his way back to the abandoned farmhouse thirty miles east of town. With the shape Jimmy in is, he'll freeze to death before he ever figures out where his feet are, let alone how to stand up on them.

"Come on, Jimmy. Let's get you up here."

He lifts Jimmy under the shoulders, but Jimmy pulls a face and Lloyd suspects one of the Fleck brothers, has been trying out their steel-toed boots on his ribs. Probably broken. He'll send Constable Pete out later to the Fleck brothers, but right now he's going to need one of his constables to help him get Jimmy into the back of the cruiser. He slides one leather glove under Jimmy's distended cheek and lays his head back down on the frozen ground.

"Back in a minute, buddy," Lloyd says.

He gets in the car, radios in, waits for a response from his detachment. All he hears is static and barely audible voices from some distant place on the same frequency, no one in particular, no answer from his own detachment. Someone must have turned the radio signal down. Perhaps his youngest, Clare, fiddling with the buttons and dials, fragmented voices, the amber, red, and green lights flickering on and off like a child's toy—despite the fact that Lloyd is a serious corporal, trying to run a stern detachment, still Jacqueline allows the children to play in the office.

He considers trying to raise St. Paul, but after yesterday's river visitor call, he can't very well raise them at this time in the morning and expect one of their constables to come out. He picks up his cigar butt from the ashtray and takes a puff, but the cigar is out. He pushes the lighter in on the dash. He could radio the ambulance, but the paramedics have had their fill of driving Jimmy out to the farmhouse only to have Jimmy show up three or nine hours later, however long it takes Jimmy to walk back into town. He doubts the paramedics would even come. No, he'll swing back to the hotel and see if he can get Neville to give him a hand. Not RCMP protocol by any means but Lloyd's small-town version of Maintiens le droit.

» » »

When Lloyd comes back, he's got Neville in the cruiser and a Styrofoam cup of hot coffee for himself, some leftover bacon and eggs and toast with margarine that Neville hurriedly wrapped in tinfoil for Jimmy.

"Where did you say he was?" Neville asks as Corporal Lloyd pulls into the Legion parking lot.

The sun is up, but you wouldn't know it by the thick band of grey that makes up the sky. Ice crystals in the still, frigid air now that the wind has died. Lloyd stops the cruiser in front of the doorway.

"He's in there," he tells Neville. "He must have rolled over or something."

Lloyd and Neville get out of the car and walk to the entrance. Jimmy is gone. Lloyd glances across the lot, sees nothing, checks the perimeter of the low brick building. No Jimmy. He shakes his head at Neville. Neville gets back into the cruiser and lights a cigarette. He deals with Jimmy on a regular basis, lets him clear the snow out front of his hotel and the café in exchange for breakfast. Sometimes Jimmy shows up, sometimes not.

Where the hell could he have gone? Lloyd checks out the

mountain of plowed snow on the other side of the lot. No one. He looks for telltale footprints, but the snow is hard and frozen; no help there. That frozen pool of blood on the cement pad where he left Jimmy lying and his leather glove is gone too. He looks up and down the empty street, then climbs back into the cruiser for warmth.

"I don't know how he managed it. He couldn't even keep his head off the ground." Lloyd cranks the heat up. "His ribs are busted all to hell too. The guy must have steel balls or something," he says, putting the cruiser into drive.

"Or wild turkeys." Neville grins and stubs his cigarette out in the ashtray.

Lloyd doesn't say anything.

"Want this?" Neville holds the leftover eggs and bacon up as Lloyd drives through the streets peering into doorways, down alleys, behind garages.

Lloyd shakes his head. Neville opens the foil and pulls out a strip of fatty bacon and eats it.

"I'll come back later and have breakfast," Lloyd says.

"I'd better get back to the hotel," Neville says, looking at his watch.

Lloyd turns the corner and stops in front of the café. Some of the early bird farmers are at the front counter.

"Bring Jimmy round, tell him I'll make sausage and pancakes," Neville says and gets out of the cruiser.

Lloyd heads down Main Street to the secondary highway to see if Jimmy's on his way home. But he's so busted up; Lloyd doesn't know how he could manage it. Maybe it's the cold or the alcohol or

23

the combination of both that enables Jimmy to pick himself up time and time again to walk back out to his father's land when he's had his fill of the town and its shadowy hospitality. Why he keeps coming back Lloyd doesn't know. Neville says Jimmy's a lost soul, hence the alcohol, the walkabouts, the strange ramblings—that Jimmy is looking for something and when he finds it, he'll know and then he'll be done with it. But Lloyd doesn't think so. He's seen it before in his small, sweet Sylvie—that inner obscure world that only she understood, and so, too, does Jimmy. It's not the Wild Turkey; it's something else entirely. Lloyd knows that Jimmy's life depends on the something else.

Wednesday, October 1987 » Lesa, age 31

Lesa struts through the Arrival doors, her rayon cape streaming/ screaming out behind, exposing her athletic legs in black Spandex. She pushes back the white hair that clings to her face with the tenacity of an octopus, pulls the John out from her pleather boots and lights it. The business-class passengers veer around her, maintaining their distance, with the exception of the good-looking man in the blue suit, standing directly behind, whom she keeps in her periphery, and in return he matches her every nonchalant glance back. She takes a deep curative drag and blows the smoke out like a 1940s film star, looks around for her brother, Nate. He's nowhere in sight, likely late as usual. Good thing he's a genius at his job (he's a corporate lawyer), otherwise no one would put up with the constant waiting. Waiting for Nate, she titles him, Waiting for Godot. As for the blue-suit man, she simply titles him Waiting. Waiting for a sign from her, perhaps?

The passengers stand around the luggage carousel, checking their watches every four seconds to see if they'll make their nine o'clock meetings. Lesa wanders over to the closed money exchange kiosk, checks the current rate on the American dollar. The Canadian dollar is winning, good for her baby sister Clare, who is no longer a baby but lethal age, stunning in her looks and in Las Vegas at the moment with a pack of friends, no doubt lounging in stringed bikinis by some glittering swimming pool downing fresh lime margaritas before the sun even begins to hit its hot desert stride.

The baggage starts down the chute. Lesa drops her John Player onto the tiled floor and grinds it with the toe of her boot, leaves it there. She catches blue-suit man watching her. Yes, waiting, she thinks, based on the pleasantly charged look on his smooth face. He's also playing hide 'n' peek with the dark-skinned child from the airplane. The child looks out from behind her mother's legs and when she sees his smiling face retreats shyly back until she can work up the courage to steal another quick look. The man smiles at the exhausted-looking mother.

Nice teeth, Lesa thinks. Obviously kind. She likes that. The man is tall, affluently dressed, definitely ex-something: hockey player, coach, professional trainer. In the early morning light his face looks closer to forty, not the fifty she had speculated on the plane. She imagines that if she wanders down the relatively empty halls of Arrivals that he might follow, follow her into the unattended stairway leading up to Departures, or the women's washroom, anywhere reasonably private.

Though she'd much prefer the get-to-know-you interface over a posh dinner that serves as foreplay, three glasses of red wine from a bona fide glass bottle, not the cardboard boxes with the plastic spigots that she's used to from her boyfriend's art show openings. But good wholehearted wine that glides down her throat, warm and smooth and heady, clouding her normally sound judgment. She feels drunk just thinking about it.

She hasn't slept much the past few nights, the anticipation of returning home so long after her father's death, so long a dearth of mothers. She swivels her stiff neck, her stomach churning from too many cups of coffee, watches for her red-zippered suitcase that matches her red-zippered purse. The man reaches for his briefcase with those hands, those boyish hands touching his black leather Samsonite, the real thing, no pleather here. And that's part of it too, beyond the palpable attraction, his apparent benevolence toward Arabic-speaking mothers and shy children, is the expense/expanse of him, the possibility that someone could transport her from this Wednesday, someone so unlike her current partner.

She's had a few partners over the course of her thirty-one years, should probably get herself a flip calendar in order to keep track of them all—though singularly, one at a time, not the habitual overlay of extramartial women that her father had over the early course of his years with her mother. Who would put up with that? Certainly not her. Still she wonders about her sculptor boyfriend, his distraction, his preoccupation with art, the openings, the art critics who cream their pants over his every exhibition: a solitary silver door suspended on a brick red wall three floors up, a suit made up entirely of flank steak, his still-in-progress burnt toast exhibit. (What does it mean? What does it say about modern society?) The constant smash of enamoured art students lounging around his studio at Emily Carr, their apartment in the West End, with their jet-black rough-cropped hair, black-mascara eyes, multi-pierced ears, their fresh, unsullied skin and slim firm bodies, male and female alike. It's a lot to keep up with some days. Not that any of that would justify this pretty man in a blue suit retrieving a briefcase made up entirely of cow; he's an extravagance she's never had, never allowed herself.

The pretty man glances over, tries to make eye contact, but she's lost in his boy-hands. She feels them on her body, her not-so-fresh but warm skin, his hands soft, kind, searching, finding something she thought she lost a long time ago. By the increasing thrum buried deep in her groin and her rabbit-quick heart, if he has to retrieve one more piece of luggage she may not need him after all.

Wednesday, July 1961 » Jacqueline, age 27

The woman from next door joins Jacqueline on the front step. She's older than Jacqueline by twelve or twenty years. It's difficult to guess by the woman's pallid, flat-cheeked face and honey-blond hair. Her husband is older too, although he's still a constable. Jacqueline's husband is writing his corporal exam next month, and with any luck they'll be transferred out to his own detachment. The woman is a foster mother, didn't or couldn't have any of her own. Jacqueline doesn't know, has never asked, but the woman always has two or more children who rotate on a regular basis. Jacqueline sees them every three or four months, and then they, like Charles the kitten, disappear. Right now her neighbour has a set of teenaged twins, a boy and a girl who go off to summer school each morning and don't usually come home until well after dark. Jacqueline says hello to them as she sits out on the front step after she's managed to get her children to bed, the red ember of her cigarette glowing in the spreading darkness; there's not much point in getting attached.

Jacqueline smiles sideways at her neighbour. Mary? Marina? Marianna? Miriam? She can never remember properly, so to be safe, she avoids the woman's name altogether.

"Would you like a cigarette?" Jacqueline offers her a Peter Jackson.

"Thank you, no," the woman says.

Jacqueline has to suppress a smile. The woman, in contrast to her dishevelled hair, and clearly wearing her husband's shirt, has the manners of a queen. Then Jacqueline remembers that she is also wearing her husband's RCMP sweatshirt. She breathes in the sweat-laden scent left by his summer skin and holds herself a moment before lighting her cigarette with a wooden match. A throng of children, hers included, although she doesn't do a head count this time around, are on the street, playing a version of kick-the-can. They run screaming to the telephone pole with the red ribbon tied around it. There must be fifteen of them now.

"How's your husband?" Jacqueline asks.

"He's fine, hoping to retire soon, but with what he makes, I don't see how we shall manage it," the woman says.

Jacqueline nods and smiles kindly.

"Perhaps the foster children," the woman adds. "As a source of income."

Jacqueline hopes her husband makes corporal next month. She's seen men older than him write their exams three, four, five times, and once they hit a certain age, the RCMP doesn't consider them anymore. She knows there aren't any hard, fast rules around that, but she suspects that once you are out of your prime like so many other things in life, if you haven't already proved yourself worthy, then your chances for career, marriage, even simple companionship taper off distinctly.

The two mothers watch the pack of children whiz across the

lawns, but the woman doesn't have a vested interest in them. Instead she gazes vacantly down the street and waits for Jacqueline to initiate the next topic.

"Will you get another kitten?" Jacqueline asks.

"Charles was such a lovely kitten, one of a kind, really. My husband was especially fond of him. The special ones are hard to replace," the woman says, looking at Jacqueline with her water-coloured eyes. So unlike Sylvie's, this woman's eyes have a definite bottom to them, a kind of thin hardness.

Jacqueline refrains from asking about the current set of twins. She remembers she has coffee brewing on the stove.

"Would you like a coffee?" she asks.

"Yes, thank you, I would," says the woman.

Jacqueline gets up and goes into the house. Inside it's so wonderfully cool and quiet, she'd like to lie down on the chesterfield for a few minutes, but of course she can't. She has a guest on the front step, a rare occurrence.

The Pyrex on the stove is bubbling gently, making soft sighing sounds like those of a satisfied woman. Jacqueline stands a moment in the kitchen and enjoys the hushed murmur of the coffee. She looks out the window, her focus somewhere off in the distance at the ravine beyond where the children are not allowed to go. She notices a car in the alley, which in itself is not unusual; certainly cars pass through the alley all the time. But the long, sage-coloured station wagon with wood panels on the sides is stopped; she can hear the motor idling in between the sound of a radio playing elsewhere, the chickadees in among the cotoneasters with their two-note refrain, first high, then low, *Be-there, Be-there*. At least that's what it always sounds like to Jacqueline, a wearisome reminder that she's running behind and she won't ever catch up. She stands on her toes to get a better look at the car and sees the familiar glint of Sylvie's black hair in the bright sun. The hair on the back of Jacqueline's neck stands on end. She feels abruptly nauseated, as if she will throw up right then and there in the kitchen sink on top of the dirty dishes leftover from breakfast and lunch that she hasn't got to yet. She feels the bile rise in her throat. She fights it back down. Not now, not now.

As if in her dreams, helpless, she watches the man at the wheel of the idling station wagon as he kicks open the passenger door with his foot. She can see him clearly in the light of day: his brown brush cut, the angle of his cheeks, she registers that the right one is scarred, the blue eyes, the startling size of his extended hand that has something in it—what, she can't tell, but Sylvie sees it and is interested. Sylvie steps toward the car door. Sylvie loves car rides. It's her favourite thing to do. Car ride? she asks whenever she sees one pass by on the street. Sylvie go car ride?

Without taking her eyes off Sylvie, Jacqueline scans the alley peripherally. Where is Lesa? Her steadfast guardian angel, Sister Lesa? Doesn't Lesa know a child's safety lies in numbers? She can't see Lesa anywhere. The man smiles widely, encouragingly. He's saying something—Sylvie's name? How can he know? Sylvie moves toward the smiling car, the idling man. If Lesa were there, Jacqueline could yell for her to get Sylvie and Sylvie would come. Jacqueline never raises her voice to Sylvie; it only causes Sylvie to run faster, farther away. She is afraid to open her mouth now at the screen window in her kitchen in the bright light of day, radios

32

playing, chickadees singing, the smell of freshly mown lawn on the slight breeze, the strange smiling man, the car, her daughter.

She's paralyzed by the fear that if she opens her mouth and a scream is what comes out, then she'll terrify Sylvie. Who knows what Sylvie might do? Jump into the passenger seat, reach for whatever the man has in his hand, or bolt, and turn and run the other direction down the alley? Oh God, if there ever was one, let there be one now. *Be-there*, the chickadees scold. *Be-there*. But Lesa's not there. She's nowhere in sight.

Sylvie takes another step forward to see what the man has in his hand. She's half in, half out of the station wagon now. Jacqueline feels the underside of her fear fall out, terror spikes through her body like an electrical charge.

"Sylvie!" she yells out the kitchen window.

Sylvie pauses, surreally, as if perched precariously at the top of the steep basement stairs over and over again like in Jacqueline's dreams. Sylvie turns from the car and grins her crooked smile back at her mother, holding up a single red Smartie, as if to say, "See, Mom, it's all right. It's just a Smartie." The man follows Sylvie's gaze to the woman in the kitchen window, and for a brief exacting moment, mother and stranger lock eyes. Then the man smiles at her too, a smile that etches itself in Jacqueline's mind like a pick-axe, so that when she tells it to the RCMP constable they send in lieu of her RCMP husband who couldn't be found at the moment, nor could they raise him on the radio, then Jacqueline will tell the husband of the woman waiting for her coffee on Jacqueline's front step right now that the man's top two middle teeth were inverted like a V, and he had a scar on his right cheek and his eyes were blue, arctic ice.

Wednesday, February 1973 » Lloyd, age 40

After checking the farmhouse for evidence of Jimmy and finding nothing, no indication that Jimmy's even been there in the last week, month, Corporal Lloyd swings back toward town, the street lights faint in the ashen, cold morning. Corporal Lloyd sees a car parked along the shoulder of the highway, half-assed in the shallow ditch, half not. The windows are covered in white rime. He doesn't recognize the silver '62 Pontiac. He slides his RCMP cruiser in behind, waits a moment, watching for movement within the car, can't see through the heavy frost. Tries to radio the licence plates in, gets the sputter of static again. Hell, he hates to approach a vehicle blind. He's going to have to outlaw the office altogether from his kids, who run freely back and forth between their attached house and the RCMP detachment like it's the Wonderful World of Walt Disney.

He pulls the zipper up on his parka, gets out of the car, and walks around the Pontiac. No vehicular damage beyond the rusted-out wheel wells, the everyday dents of car door dings along the side panels. No damage to the front or rear bumpers. He peers into the back window of the Pontiac, can't see inside. Fishes out his wallet, digs around for the "Kleenex" of credit cards, so familiar his handy-dandy Chargex, a household name, which he uses to cover the constant shortfall of his meagre RCMP salary: the credit card both curse and blessing. He clears a small patch on the car window with the plastic edge. Cups his one leather glove (he *lent* the other to Jimmy) around the patch, peers in, is greeted by a multitude of wide eyes. His jolt almost imperceptible, not what he expected: occupants alive, five children pressed together in the back seat for warmth, the baby has no shoes on, all flat-eyed and peering out the icy car at him.

For Chrissakes, who the hell's in charge here?

He straightens up a moment, surveys the flat white prairies, exhales visibly in the cold February air, tries the car door, opens it slowly, carefully, so as not to scare the children. They stare out at him, their breath also visible, white, flat like the light in their eyes, the prairie landscape. All under the age of seven, Lloyd guesses. Three of them have on summer coats, the toddler is wrapped in a tat-tered Hudson's Bay blanket, the shoeless baby has no socks. Corporal Lloyd removes his glove, smiles, reaches in to check the baby's pale cheeks for life, warmth; the other children lean away from him.

"It's okay," he says. "Hungry?"

The oldest boy nods, the younger ones stare at him.

The baby's cheeks barely warm.

"Best to cover this one up," he says, taking the baby from the girl in the orange flowered summer jacket. The toothless baby smells like cardamom. He unzips his parka, tucks the baby inside, feels her bare glacial feet through the layers of his pressed beige shirt and cotton undershirt. Holding the baby against his chest, Lloyd leans into the front seat. The driver, male, approximately thirty years old, is slumped over the steering wheel. The female in the passenger seat is leaning against the window. No blood apparent on the apparent parents: no injuries, no wounds, no impairment that Lloyd can make out other than impaired; the fusty smell of last night's alcohol strong inside the closed car. The dull eyes of children like impending victims.

"Parents?" Corporal Lloyd asks.

The older boy responds with an indeterminate nod. The toddler in the Hudson Bay blanket puts her arms out to be lifted.

Lloyd presses his lips together in a straight line, surveys the aberrant mother, glances over at the father in the driver's seat passed out over the steering wheel, a line of still spit pooled on the man's bottom lip, his five children in the back seat—Lloyd knows paradox like the back of his gloveless hand.

His Jacqueline at home holding down the fort; he is enormously glad for that; he probably needs to tell her that or buy her roses or something. He thanks God for the stable women, not like this one in the front seat.

One by one, he coaxes the children out of the silver Pontiac into the cruiser where he's cranked the heater up full. He tries to convince one or two of the children to sit in the front, but the older boy insists they all sit in the back. Corporal Lloyd takes his parka off, wraps the cardamom-scented baby in it, and passes her to the girl in the orange coat. The girl grins shyly, a row of white baby teeth. He radios in once more, manages to raise Constable Pete, who responds in a thick morning voice.

"About time," Corporal Lloyd says.

"The volume was turned off," says Constable Pete.

Corporal Lloyd shakes his head, relays his location, the situation. "I need you to come out here and haul these—"

Dumb asses is what Lloyd is thinking; he glances in the rear-view mirror, five pairs of child eyes watching his every move.

"*Parents* back to the holding cell," he says.

"Find out who the heck they are," he says to Constable Pete. "And call Social Services in Edmonton, they'll want to know about this. And next of kin too. And when you're done that, go looking for Jimmy Widman. He's in rough shape."

"What are you doing?" Constable Pete asks.

"We're going for pancakes," Lloyd says, puts the flashing lights on for fun, drives wordlessly down the highway to Neville's hotel. He glances at the clock, nearly 9:00 AM, his shift almost done; the price of a quiet month on this breathless Wednesday morning.

Wednesday, October 1987 » Lesa, age 31

She spots her brother, Nate, by the baggage carousel. He's spotted her too. She's hard to miss in her Storm getup, but he doesn't know it's her. She walks directly toward him. He moves in the other direction as if scanning the revolving carousel for luggage he doesn't have. Lesa follows along behind him, almost on his heels, waiting for him to turn and tell her off, which, of course, Nate would never do. The other passengers are enormously interested, especially blue-suit man. Nate picks up his pace. Lesa stops.

"Nate!" she says.

Nate turns and recognizes Lesa's pale face beneath the white hair. Lesa stands on her toes. God, she's forgotten how tall he is, six-foot-five at least. Dark hair like their father, like Sylvie. She throws her arms around Nate's skinny neck.

"Of course that had to be you," Nate says, his face flushing.

"Oh, Nate!" Lesa lets go of him and play punches him in the belly. Nate doesn't respond.

The passengers go back to their business of luggage retrieval. Blue-suit man cocks his head to one side, watching her. He is waiting. She lights another cigarette, glances up at Nate, who is scowling at her filthy habits: cigarettes, inappropriate airport attire, white synthetic hair, burnt toast boyfriends. She inhales her John Player Special, wishes she were special herself, a player like blue-suit man. Forget Nate, forget her waiting mother, her dead father. She wishes the man would come across the marbled floor of the airport and transport her, take her somewhere she's never been before with his smooth boy-hands, even though she has no idea who he is—but in this fractured moment, she's with him. No past, present, or future, simply the split second of the here and now, this beautiful, fucked-up, transitory moment that she needs to hang on to. She understands her father absolutely.

"Who's that?" Nate asks.

The two men watch each other.

"No one," Lesa says, puts her burning face in her hands, peeks out at the man through her fingers like the dark-skinned child, only Lesa's is a carnal game of hide 'n' find. She presses her lips together in a straight, sad line, shakes her head. She is no player. The man salutes her, picks up his leather Samsonite, and goes out to hail one of the fifty identical black cars waiting alongside the airport curb. Lesa watches him go; Nate watches her.

Lesa exhales a last drag out the side of her mouth, then drops the butt onto the floor. She spots her red multi-zippered bag on the carousel and goes to claim it. Nate extinguishes her cigarette butt with the heel of his politician-helper shoes, size fifteen, hard to find; he buys three pairs at a time. He throws the flattened butt into the ashtray.

"Ready?" Nate says.

"Never ready," Lesa says.

Nate looks at her, smiles, perhaps from relief, perhaps from her passing storm.

Lesa hefts her suitcase into the back of her non-driving mother's Toyota. She notices something tucked beneath the outside strap of her suitcase. Scrawled across an Air Canada vomit bag: *For a good time call* 247-2614 ☺. Thank fuck, she thinks and stuffs the paper bag inside her purse.

Wednesday, July 1961 » Jacqueline, age 27

"Who is that?" Lesa comes into the kitchen, asks in a breathy whisper about the RCMP officer who isn't her father but the constable from next door. Jacqueline shoos her back into the living room to watch Bugs Bunny with Nate, but Lesa doesn't go. Instead she stands at the door and watches them at the kitchen table.

"Lesa, go out of this room now," Jacqueline says, rising from her orange vinyl chair, her anger also rising unreasonably.

Lesa's face crumbles as if she might cry, but Jacqueline's fierceness keeps her in check. Keeps Jacqueline from interrogating Lesa. Where were you? How could you let your sister run around by herself? *You-weren't-there.* Jacqueline knows she's not rational at the moment: Lesa's five, for God's sake. The girl is only five. She hadn't realized how much she relied on Lesa's help where Sylvie was concerned, *but down the back alley, alone?*

Lesa's chin quivers and Jacqueline knows if she were a good mother, a capable mother, a mother who could *be-there* in order to keep her children safe, then she would go over and pull Lesa into her hip and run her long, curled fingernails through Lesa's strawberry hair and tell her it's all right, honey, everything is all right. But her legs aren't steady and if she lets go of her chair, she'll collapse into a heap on the kitchen floor. She can't risk that. Lesa goes back into the living room.

Jacqueline sits down. The officer pulls out his small black book. Where is my husband? Jacqueline wants to ask. Why can't he be reached by phone, radio? How is it possible that no one seems to know where he is? She's never had to contact him at work before, and perhaps this is the norm, but still she finds it surreal that even the RCMP can't track him down when she needs him most. She relays the details that have imbedded themselves in her mind, playing over and over like a looped film reel: a station wagon, sage with wood panels, eyes blue, hard blue, hands large, scar on his right cheek, inverted V on top teeth. No, she didn't get the licence plate. Yes, he said her name. No, she didn't hear him, she *saw* him. Sylvie, he said. She's sure of that, dreadfully sure.

When Jacqueline yelled out the kitchen window the station wagon sped off, knocking Sylvie to the ground. Jacqueline ran straight into the alley and tackled Sylvie before she could regain herself and possibly take off running. She held Sylvie tight in her arms, so tight that instead of the usual squirming and flailing like Sylvie did whenever Jacqueline tried to hold her, Sylvie relinquished, relaxed uncharacteristically into her mother's arms—a rare but fundamental hug on the gravel in the forbidden back alley.

Sylvie opened her small sweaty fist and showed Jacqueline the red Smartie that *that man*, Sylvie called him, she pointed down the alley to a churned-up cloud of dust, had given her. The adrenalin that ripped through Jacqueline's body not four minutes ago turned instead to a crushing exhaustion. She sat and rocked in the back alley with Sylvie in her arms for as long as Sylvie would allow, eerily void of emotion, as if the *dis*-ease that coursed through Jacqueline's veins over the days, weeks, months took over and released her from her responsibilities. Then the two of them got up and walked back into the row of identical houses.

Now, here at the kitchen table, Sylvie picks up different colours of Smarties from the bowl Jacqueline set out in order to keep her still and safe. Sylvie shows the Smarties to Jacqueline and the officer. When she picks up the red one, Jacqueline feels like throwing up again, takes a sharp breath to keep herself in check. Everything is about order, Jacqueline reasons in her mind. In order to keep Sylvie occupied, in order to keep her children safe, in order to combat the broken feeling that is welling up in her as she answers the officer's questions. After this she must get the dishes done, prepare dinner, put the laundry away in order to get through to this evening when her husband comes home. She knows she can't rely on him, but she can't bring herself to think beyond this evening to tomorrow morning when the world will begin all over again, fresh with danger.

She looks at the officer and notices, despite his age, he's firm-bodied, slightly handsome. His face is strangely unscathed, innocent even in contrast to his job, his constable status, and the state of his dishevelled wife next door and their revolving door of foster children. Odd that she never noticed this before. She doesn't know why she notices it now, but he is sitting at her kitchen table and her husband is nowhere to be found and she finds that she needs some *body*, any *body*.

"Have you seen the man before around the neighbourhood, perhaps? The supermarket? Anywhere that you can recall?" the officer asks.

"No, nowhere. I don't know how he knew her name." Jacqueline pulls out a cigarette from her pack, and the officer steadies her shaking hand by cupping it with his own so she can light it. She offers him one.

"No, thank you," he says.

He closes his black notebook and gets up. He stands a moment, gazing at Sylvie, who offers him a warmed Smartie from the palm of her hand.

"Thank you," he says, taking the Smartie, but he doesn't put it into his mouth. Instead he tucks the tacky Smartie into the breast pocket of his uniform.

"For later," he says and pats Sylvie on the head as if she were his own.

Jacqueline doesn't take her eyes off Sylvie to look at the officer. She's afraid of what she might do.

"Mary-Lynn can stop by later if you like," the officer says.

Jacqueline looks up, confused, then realizes he's talking about his wife, her next-door neighbour whose name she can't ever remember. She nods, fixes her eyes back on Sylvie; in fact, she can't take her eyes off Sylvie. She's terrified if she does, then something in her will break and she won't be able to pick up the pieces to make dinner for her three children.

Wednesday, February 1973 » Lloyd, age 40

Neville flips pancakes high into the air, then onto the plates lined up across the grill. Neville's 9:00 AM audience: two retired dairy farmers that come in every morning in lieu of milking cows, birthing calves, talking to their wives. Three bearded, black-clad men from the Hutterite colony. Eve, the hairless owner of Eve's Beauty Salon across the street who's undergoing chemo treatments for lung cancer, smokes her cigarettes through a long-handled holder. Five wide-eyed children with front-row seats at Neville's counter, and the blond stranger from the bar last night sitting solo in the corner booth.

Lloyd swivels on his stool, the baby girl in his arms, runs his eyes over the blonde, who returns a Wonderful Wide World of White Teeth; she waves at the baby with one finger. Lloyd smiles at the blonde, the irony. Short of abandoning the children, who aren't his, which the parents have already done, Lloyd can't do much but watch the woman slip away and put the moves on the only other eligible male in the place: Neville, not particularly catching in looks with his black oiled hair, prerequisite cook's belly overhanging his skillet-sized belt buckle, a slap-me-go-lucky grin on his face this morning due to the blonde. On the whole, Neville is partial neither to blondes nor brunettes nor redheads but partial in general to any willing woman.

Neville sets the plates down in front of the row of children; the older ones don't even stop to breathe before diving into the happy-face pancakes, hungry-face kids.

"Jimmy turn up yet?" Neville asks.

Lloyd shakes his head.

"He will, always does."

"That's the hope," Lloyd says.

He turns back to the counter to cut up the sausages and pancakes for the Hudson's Bay toddler swivelling on the red stool beside him.

Neville whistles the American anthem in Smoky Lake, Alberta, Canada, as he scrapes the grill.

"O, say can you see by the blonde's early light?" He sings.

The fatty smell of fried eggs and bacon grease, glass pots of black coffee like burnt asphalt on the silver hotplates above, cigarette smoke drifting from dented metal ashtrays on the tables, from Eve, from the blonde in the corner booth, Lloyd's cigar smoke mixing, fusing in the familial air of Neville's café. Lloyd knows Neville hasn't got a chance if Lloyd decides first he wants the blond stranger for later. But somehow the blonde doesn't seem to matter this morning with a clutch of half-starved children at the counter, a baby cooing in his arms sucking on a piece of buttered toast, a babbling toddler beside him, her round mouth filled with maple pancakes. Lloyd watches Neville stride genially around the café wiping tables, clearing dishes, filling coffee cups. The two farmers, three Hutterites, Eve respond with raised eyebrows at Neville's never-before attentiveness—anything to bask in the early light of the blond beauty in the corner.

Lloyd thinks instead of Jacqueline at home, drifting through her long days in a brightly coloured kaftan, Lesa and Nate and Clare whirling around the house, the attached detachment. Jacqueline, his steady Betty, which is what his mother called Jacqueline for the first two years they were married—Betty, an old girlfriend of Lloyd's who his mother thought he should have married. Jacqueline gets the short end of the stick, the short straw of his mother, a double whammy. Lloyd knows he could be a better husband too. He puffs on his El Producto cigar, takes a long, slow sip of the scorched coffee.

Neville loiters at the table next to the blonde's booth, chatting her up. The blonde responds with dark flashing eyes, those striking white teeth. She glances past Neville at Lloyd, a soft look in her eyes, too bad so sad on her crimson lips. Or is it? Lloyd looks steadily at the blonde, his own dark eyes flickering, then past her out the café window. Ice glittering like glass shards on the north wind, the grey light of morning, the grey pigeons seeking refuge beneath the eaves of the hardware store across the street next to hairless Eve's. Despite the live wire he can feel burning, sending out shocks beneath his skin, despite the Crown Royal he craves after his shift that burns uniformly down his throat, makes him salivate like Pavlov's dog. Despite the sweet wild aftertaste of a woman that rouses the tip of his penis, stirs deep in his groin; Lloyd makes the choice not to partake this time. Leaves her to Neville. A hotel owner goes a long way in a small town, doesn't it? The blonde's eyes go back to Neville. Apparently so.

Wednesday, October 1987 » Lesa, age 31

Nate stops the car in front of their mother's house. The house is dark. Never-ready Lesa is thankful; she's not ready to go inside yet.

"Think she's up?" Lesa asks.

Nate shrugs.

"Don't know why she would be at . . ." Lesa glances at the clock on the dashboard. "7:22 AM."

Nate looks at Lesa.

"You could at least take the Storm wig off," he says.

Lesa touches the synthetic hair.

"Later."

Nate rolls his eyes, gets out of the car. Lesa knows Nate doesn't get her. Why her boyfriend is a sculptor (akin to being a poet or a street busker, in the subterranean vault of the human food chain as far as Nate's concerned.) Or why her hair is cropped blunt and shorter even than Nate's. Or why she celebrates the hallow eve of her father's death while Nate mourns it. Or why she resurrects Sylvie when all everyone else would like to do is forget forget forget.

"You know what?" Lesa squares her cape across her shoulders. "I'm going to go get us a couple coffees."

"I'll come with you," Nate says.

"Not now, Nate," Lesa says.

"What do you want me to tell her?" Nate sighs, stands by the car with that lost-little-boy look on his face that Lesa remembers from when Sylvie went away for good and didn't come back. It was months before Nate quit asking their mother where she was. Lesa didn't need to ask.

"Tell her my flight was delayed. Tell her I don't get in until this afternoon. Tell her there's a storm warning."

She flashes a smile at Nate.

Nate doesn't react. Lesa knows he's used to her sudden recklessness.

"I'll tell her you borrowed the car and you might bring it back in one piece," Nate says.

Lesa climbs over the console, blows Nate a kiss. In the rear-view mirror, she sees him still standing on the curb, his beige coat flapping in the cold fall wind as she drives down the silent street her mother lives on; Nate's shoulders slumped, his long arms hanging limp, helpless at his side.

She recalls a Second Cup in the vicinity of her mother's house. She keeps driving north, farther north than necessary. *North to Alaska*, she sings in her head. North-by-northwest will take her to where Sylvie is. Where Lesa hasn't been since they were both children; nonetheless, Sylvie is there like some sharp pebble from a residual playground in Lesa's Hush Puppies/Adidas/stiletto boots— a problematic reminder of something she must do, something she needs to finish once and for all. What that is, Lesa doesn't know. She only knows it's there along with the piercing pebble of her/their youth, along with Sylvie's soft chatter in her mind, in Lesa's wandering days and purposeless nights at her casino job on Davie Street while her boyfriend is at his studio on Water Street, black-clad fan club et al.

She passes the Second Cup without stopping, joins the early morning rush-hour traffic on John Laurie, meanders slowly east past Fourth, then Centre Street, where most of the cars drop off and head south to downtown while she continues on. She hasn't really thought about where she's going other than simply away.

She merges north on Deerfoot, pulls the white wig off, runs her fingernails lightly through her hair like her mother used to when she was a kid. She wishes she were a kid again. That brief period in time when no matter what, all is forgiven; everything slips away like silk to skin, smoke to air, a magician's *trick* performed by her mother. This last thought forming goose-bumps along the surface of Lesa's freckled skin beneath the black Spandex. She knows the *trick* of the dysfunctional family only too well in that it leaves you lacking, looking for something that doesn't exist. A kind of neatly packaged perfection she might find only in Samsonite luggage and smooth-handed strangers. She knows also the illusionary *trick* of memory: the curvature of her mother's long nails like the curve of mother earth itself running through her child hair. The jasmine scent of her mother's Chanel No. 5 mixed with the dark of her Peter Jacksons, the present chill in the October air.

Lesa lights a cigarette, feels the nicotine slip down her throat, fill her lungs, and then deeper she imagines, along the cylindrical walls of her veins where her blood also runs quick and deep and dark.

Wednesday, July 1961 » Jacqueline, age 27

Jacqueline looks at the gold spiral clock on the living room wall. It's half past three. The dishes are done, laundry put away, pork chops are thawing on the Arborite countertop in the kitchen. Jacqueline managed to cajole Sylvie and Nate down into the cool basement to play Lego, or at least watch Sylvie play Lego. No one else is allowed to when Sylvie is present, only in Jacqueline's dreams does Sylvie share. Nate runs up and down the stairs retrieving his Hot Wheels cars two at a time from the living room, one in each of his chubby three-year-old hands. Lesa hasn't surfaced from her bedroom since the officer left. Jacqueline starts down the hall to check on her, but again, like in the kitchen, she feels an irrational rage that she knows she can't inflict on Lesa. She stands in the middle of the room, paralyzed. Should she call her husband again? What if he still can't be reached? Surely they are doing everything they can to contact him? She's not sure she can stand to hear that he's unavailable at the moment and would she care to leave a message? She puts her hands over her face, but then Nate thumps up the wood stairs again and stops, watching her. She wipes her face and reins herself in.

"Would you like some cheese slices and apple?" she asks.

Nate nods.

"Go back downstairs and I'll bring some."

Nate disappears into the basement.

Jacqueline goes into the kitchen. She's got all the doors and windows locked. The house is stifling. She slides the kitchen window open slightly while she peels apples over the sink. Outside the sun is directly overhead, the height of the afternoon heat. The air is dense and muggy, like before a thunderstorm. She avoids looking into the alley; she can still see the station wagon idling in her mind's eye, Sylvie in the back seat waving merrily goodbye as the car disappears into the transparent waves of heat rising off the gravel. She looks instead to the sky in the west; sure enough, it's darkening, preparing for something. She recalls the huge red sun on the horizon this morning. Really, could it only have been this morning? The day feels like months. She remembers: Red sky at night, Sailor's delight, red sky in morning, early warning. Storm warning. Had she known, she would have locked herself and the children safely in the house for the day and made Play-Doh on the stovetop, or built Lego castles, or finger-painted, or drawn stick people in a row and cut them out and hung them like a regular family across the span of their living room wall.

The doorbell rings. Jacqueline slides the kitchen window shut and goes into the living room. She parts the drawn curtains and peers out. It's the officer from next door. He must have forgotten something, or perhaps he's got news to tell her. She opens the door and lets him in. He stands in the living room without saying anything.

"Is everything all right?" Jacqueline asks.

The officer avoids her eyes.

"Did you find him, *that man?*"

Oh, God, she sounds like Sylvie now.

"No," the officer says.

"Is it my husband, is my husband all right?" Jacqueline asks, bewildered.

Why is he making her guess?

"Your husband is fine." The officer reaches out and puts his hand lightly on her shoulder. She looks him in the eye. She knows they are trained to do this. Reach out and touch someone before delivering the bad news.

"No," he says, sensing her body tense up. "It's not that."

"Where is he?" Jacqueline asks. "Where is my husband? How do you know he's all right?"

The officer takes his hand off her shoulder and looks at her directly.

"He's indisposed," he says. "I don't know where. I tried to find him. A few of the guys at the office thought they might know . . ."

He stops.

"He's MIA," he says, no smirk, no pun.

Jacqueline regards the officer for a moment, notes the depth of his green eyes. She doesn't ask why or how, nor does her face crumble or her chin quiver. She knows. Her heart, her belly, her groin; in some distant past she's always known. *Dis*-loyal. But her *dis*-ease is strong, stronger than even this understanding, her salvation of sorts. Where it was sporadic before, now it reaches systematically inside and shuts her down like a light burning too long into the night, a slow gas leak from the kitchen stove. She reaches up impulsively and puts her arms around the officer's neck. His smell is alarmingly different than her husband's, not in a bad way, but different, earthy like dirt, so she is immediately aware of the consequences of her actions, but she's not thinking right now.

She needs to know she's present, accounted for, alive in the moment. It doesn't matter if the officer pulls her body against his, if she feels the round metal buttons of his uniform pressing into her unfettered breasts beneath her husband's sweatshirt, the thick leather of his gun holster straining in opposition to her left hip, his hands on her shoulders, her back, her thighs. None of that matters in this primal moment. She simply needs someone. Anyone. She feels his hands on her back, making small circles, gestures of comfort. She holds him taut, waiting for him to release her, but he doesn't. He lets her hold him in this way while she clings to him like a starfish to a stone. She inhales the summer damp of his skin beneath his uniform like the sea itself: close, humid, salty as she lightly kisses his neck, thankful for his civility. Then she releases him and he stands before her as though nothing had happened.

He's not so much older than her, she realizes as she surveys his unmoving, tanned face, but old enough to know what it's like to stand at the edge of a high bluff, your losses circling below you like alligators waiting for your downward plunge. The officer watches her carefully. She sees no lust, no carnal knowledge on his lined face, nothing but the shared loss in the shape of children, your own, other people's forgotten children, kittens, jobs, lives, spouses.

Jacqueline glances down the hallway and sees Lesa standing there.

"Lesa," Jacqueline says, tilting her head, once, gratefully toward the officer as he makes his way to the front door, then leaves. The quiet click of Lesa's bedroom door as she shuts her mother out. The metal burrs that form beneath the surface of Jacqueline's mother-skin.

Lloyd drives the kids out to the Métis Crossing to their aunt's house. The house is small, a *Please Take Your Shoes Off* sign scrawled on a piece of blue-lined paper at the back door. Lloyd bends down, baby in arms, struggles to unlace his brown Strathcona boots, sets them neatly on the hand-woven mat in the corner. A spattered black and orange cat that looks as if Jackson Pollock painted it sniffs the leathers of his boots, swarms Lloyd's legs.

The rest of the children have already removed their shoes, scattered through the house and disappeared. No doubt they've spent some time here. Lloyd stands in the middle of the living room holding the baby, surveys the aunt in the wheelchair, the immaculately groomed poodle in the woman's lap, a pink bow in the dog's caramel-floss hair. No furniture to speak of, save for the wheelchair, the single rocker, and a yellow marbled table in the kitchen with two chrome-legged chairs like Lloyd's mother had in the 1950s. Lloyd nods at the aunt: early fifties, he speculates. She doesn't seem surprised, smiles back at him toothless like the baby, the remedial smell of infirmity about her person.

"Mind if I look around?" Lloyd asks.

She gestures to make himself at home.

A couple mattresses tucked into the corners of a couple bedrooms in the back of the house. Downstairs the basement cement, bare wood framing. The kids piled together on some blankets watching cartoons on a small black and white television. Lloyd pauses, watches Dudley Do-right on the television struggle to untie his sweetheart from the railway tracks, a theme played out over and over again on *The Rocky and Bullwinkle Show*, in Lloyd's job, his life, present moment included, endless, he thinks. He winks at the kids, the oldest boy smiles.

Upstairs is the heavy, rich scent of game meat simmering on the stove. Lloyd peers into the pot, a large chunk of dark meat inside. The counter tops are clear, clean, immaculate, no alcohol insight.

"Husband?" asks Lloyd.

"Not today," the aunt says, a slight smile on her lip.

Lloyd isn't sure how to take that. A pot of coffee on the counter that the aunt offers him, but he's had four too many already. He looks around the sparse room, the lone woman in the wheelchair, her poodle. Yes, he decides, he does need one more. The aunt points at a cupboard, Lloyd shifts the baby to his other arm, opens the cupboard, pulls out a mug.

"You?" he asks.

She nods. He pours two cups, stirs a spoon of sugar into hers, and sits with the baby at the kitchen table while he drinks his.

"You have children?" Lloyd asks.

She shakes her head, references the two kitchen chairs.

"Are these kids your sister's?" asks Lloyd .

"Yes," she says, no opinion on her face.

"Can you manage the baby?" he asks, unwrapping his coat from around the sleeping child. He isn't as concerned about the other children. They seem used to managing. Yes, she can manage the baby; the older ones will help.

"Social Services will be coming," says Lloyd.

The aunt nods, again no surprise, no opinion. Lloyd looks around. Outside the living room window slim poplars have been strung together in an open fort structure, the tan skin of a deer hanging amid the slow, curling smoke in the cold white air.

"Recent?" he asks.

"Last week," she says. "Take some, it's in the freezer by the back door."

Lloyd sifts around in his parka pockets for something to give her, jostling the baby as he does. The baby smiles in her sleep. All he comes up with are three cellophane-wrapped cigars from Neville's lounge last night, the slim kind, tipped in rum. He hands them to the aunt, along with the sleeping baby. The aunt smiles toothlessly, shamelessly, thanks Lloyd for his kindness, her nieces and nephews, the rum-tipped cigars.

At the door Lloyd pulls his boots on, laces them up while the aunt watches. When Lloyd turns to wave, she points at the large white freezer next to the door. He opens it, finds the freezer full of brown wrapped packages, pulls one out.

"Take more," the aunt says. "The meat is rich, good. You have children?"

"Yes," Lloyd says. "Three."

He doesn't count Sylvie. She hasn't lived at home for more than a decade now. He can't remember if he ever counted her

"Tell your wife to soak it in sweet milk, less wild that way." The aunt's lips curve.

Lloyd retrieves another small package from the freezer, nods at the aunt.

The aunt doesn't see him; her attention already turned to the sleeping baby.

Outside in his cruiser, Lloyd sits a moment in the quiet space, the still of the sparse land, the spare house. Nothing much to look at, he thinks, but more than meets his eye. This stripped-down world so different than his, the woman inside so far removed from the marginal few that wander in to spend their days staggering around town until Lloyd or one of his constables pick them up, drive them home or, like this morning, back to his detachment to spend the daylight hours in the drunk tank. But for the towns-people who see only those few gone adrift that wreak havoc on the rest of the barrel; they are erroneous ambassadors. He's guilty of adrift himself, of mistaken opinions. Not like the fifty-some-year-old, toothless woman in the wheelchair with a groomed poodle and a slumbering baby in her arms, a freezer full of deer, a basement full of children whom she will look after until her sister and brother-in-law return home, return to themselves. She's the fort holder, the one who strings it all together when things go sideways, askew. Lloyd knows the world needs more people like that, like the warm, steady core of his Jacqueline. He doesn't know why she stays with him, but he knows why he stays with her. He fishes his cigar butt out of the ashtray, relights it, puts the cruiser in gear, and drives off the reserve.

Wednesday, October 1987 » Lesa, age 31

North now of the oil-affluent city readying itself for the Olympics only a few months away, the buzz of hurried construction, overhead cranes, closed-off roadways, the prairie city sprawls for miles in all directions in Lesa's rear-view mirror. Lesa amid the cars, the truckers, the farmer/ranchers barrelling down the black highway in their Chev/Dodge/GMC pick-up trucks and horse trailers. Lesa turns the radio on, scrolls through the stations till she finds, amazingly(!), Bauhaus. The black-clad, emaciated Peter Murphy singing "Bela Lugosi's Dead" and on the brown prairies no less. His deep, sonorous voice fills the airless void of her mother's Toyota Camry.

Lesa glances at herself in the rear-view mirror, touches the newly dyed sheen of her jet-black hair like Sylvie's was as a kid, the black cape tied around her neck. She isn't sure what her intent is, just knows that neither her mother nor Nate has seen her hair yet, and with it the matter of Sylvie. Always that. Regardless, she cranks the radio, accelerates, digs through her purse for a peppermint, finds instead the Air Canada vomit bag and pulls it out, chants the phone number along with Peter Murphy's *undead undead undead.* She wishes she were. The phone number is local, perhaps there's still time to play. She doesn't fly out until tomorrow afternoon. Although she doesn't see how with the dinner, her mother, Nate. She wishes her younger sister, Clare, was going to be there. She's undead and in parties in Las Vegas at the moment. Too bad, Lesa thinks. She likes Clare a lot. Even though Lesa was only six, she remembers her mother bringing mild-mannered, happy-go-baby Clare home. Her delicate features, the small round of her lightly speckled face that made Lesa press her cheek alongside Clare's until Clare got older, lost patience, and squirmed free, wanting instead to see the world for herself, not Lesa's guided version.

Clare gave their mother a reason to roust herself out of bed in the morning again. For months after Sylvie left, and before Clare was born, their mother scarcely came out of her bedroom, and if she did, it was to wander through the house in her Tang-coloured nightgown that was tight around her still-pregnant belly in search of matches to light her cigarette or perhaps burn the row housing down. Lesa didn't know which. Or her mother would spend entire vacant days on the sofa in front of the television, as long as a box of wooden matches lasted, getting up only to find more. She would fly off the handle about the toys on the living room floor, or dirty dishes left on the coffee table. A stray bobby pin on the kitchen counter-top could throw her into a sudden rage. Directed always at Lesa, never Nate, and later certainly not baby Clare. Lesa thought it had something to do with her being the oldest, or with Sylvie. Their father, of course, was still alive, but Lesa doesn't recall him being at home much, even less so once Sylvie was gone.

Peter Murphy's voice fades out. Lesa turns the radio off, tucks the vomit bag in the glove compartment. She scans the horizon,

61

the smaller surrounding town of Airdrie fades away, leaving nothing other than the wide open lowlands that are yellow, flat, outwardly tedious, but above that a prairie sky so immense/intense blue that anything might be possible. A sky she could lose herself in.

Wednesday, July 1961 » Jacqueline, age 27

Jacqueline knocks softly on Lesa's bedroom door. No answer. She knows Lesa is not asleep, not in this heat, not this early, it's only 4:30 AM. She's likely waiting incommunicado on the other side of the wood door, having removed both of the already loosened glass knobs so Jacqueline can't get in.

"Lesa, please come out and talk to me." Jacqueline breathes against the door, trying to calm her quickened heart.

Nothing.

"Lesa, Mommy has a surprise for you. We can make cookies together," Jacqueline says, even though the idea of turning on the gas oven in this heat is preposterous.

"We'll make peanut butter or chocolate chip, if you like. Come on out, I'll meet you in the kitchen."

Jacqueline stands in the dim hall, listening, the silence nearly unbearable. If she stays a minute longer, she might simply kick the door down and then she doesn't know what will happen. She is amazed at how she teeters from the void to rage with nothing in between. She walks into the sweltering kitchen and pours herself a black cup of coffee. She sits down at the table and lights a Peter

Jackson. Ridiculous to bribe a five-year-old, she knows, but she just wants to explain to Lesa about Sylvie, about life and need and want, how much she misses her husband, however diminutive all this may seem. She waits five, ten, twenty-seven minutes over the course of two cigarettes and her cup of coffee, but Lesa doesn't come.

She looks at the telephone and, in a wave of bravery, picks up the receiver and dials the RCMP office.

"RCMP. How may I help you?" a woman asks.

Jacqueline recognizes the voice as Teresa, whom she met last year at the RCMP annual Christmas ball. Teresa had on a full-length taffeta dress, cream-coloured like a not-so-new bride might choose or an opera singer would wear, her creamy cleavage on display like a Sunday buffet. She recalls they laughed together over an off-colour joke that one of the officers told the commanding officer's wife.

"Teresa?" Jacqueline says.

"Yes?"

"Has anyone been able to reach my husband?"

Teresa pauses, exhales audibly over the telephone. Teresa knows, the whole damn office probably knows. Why is the wife always the last to find out? Jacqueline's face burns red on the other side of town with the heat and shame and humiliation.

"Teresa?"

"I'm sorry we've been unable to reach him at the moment. Would you care to leave a message?"

Jacqueline doesn't answer. How can she? What could she possibly say that would make this reparable? Yes, I know my husband is momentarily indisposed in his infidelity. And you do too. Has he slept with you yet? she wants to ask Taffeta Teresa.

"Any message?" Teresa says.

"None," Jacqueline says and quietly replaces the receiver.

Wednesday, February 1973 » Lloyd, age 40

The snow is falling in large white flakes—the kind that blanket Smoky Lake, cover the desolate prairies all around, soften the North Saskatchewan River momentarily, make Lloyd's town seem gentler, kinder, if only for a short while—the kind of snowflakes his kids like. He gets a vision of young Sylvie, her dark, crooked eyes, her outstretched pink tongue catching white flakes, the seal-bark thrill of her laughter. The thought makes him hollow. He can't remember the last time he saw Sylvie, can hardly hold the picture of her in his mind anymore. Doesn't know if he could pick her out of the rash of people that were admitted in the 1950s and 1960s to the government-run Michener institution. His small, sweet Sylvie housed in the severe two-storey brick buildings laid out on sprawling grounds in precise rows like an army base along with fourteen hundred other patients, unwanted, discarded, placed, and forgotten. Or so it seemed at the time. The windows barred, doors locked from the inside, thirty-odd people crowded into a small day room, one caregiver in their midst. Difficult choices in those days for challenged clients, the equally challenged parents.

Not unwanted, or discarded, certainly not forgotten, Sylvie

always on his mind, beneath his skin. But his Sylvie placed where she could be cared for medically, properly, safely. Lloyd watched as Jacqueline, pregnant at the time with Clare, and Lesa led skipping Sylvie hand in hand through the barred doors of the institution while Lloyd stood outside in the chill of the autumn air, the culling of his children. Three-year-old Nate at his side, gazing up at him, no comprehension on his face. Lloyd couldn't bring himself to step inside the institution. He knows that betrayal was worse than any other woman. He pushes the image from his mind, watches the swirling snow all around him bend everything white.

As he drives toward town, he notices something on the highway. A blanket, clothing, perhaps? He can't tell, can barely make out the road let alone the bright red something poking through the thick snow. Farther on a dark pile almost completely covered, farther still he makes out the snowy shape of boots? He thinks about the Fleck brothers always cleaving down the highway to and from town, the back of their pickup filled with work clothes, tool boxes, muddy boots, cases of beer, them fool selves. He catches a larger shape in his periphery as he passes, swollen by the snow on the side of the road. He glances in the rear-view mirror. Likely roadkill: deer, moose, coyote, but that doesn't explain the series of snow-covered piles on the highway.

He slows his cruiser, doesn't really want to stop, wants to go home instead, fall with pounding head, mindless into his double bed. Could be a simple case of negligence, the Fleck brothers spewing their jetsam all over his highway, then hitting a deer and not bothering to report it. He watches the swollen shape disappear in his mirror, go white like everything else on the austere landscape.

But duty calls the better of him. He pulls the cruiser around, doubles back down the highway, squinting out the windshield through the falling snow until he spots the swollen dark shape beneath the landed snow. He stops, pulls on his one glove, gets out of the car, walks over to the shape, and squats beside it. Lloyd realizes it's no animal, not roadkill, but something else entirely. He brushes the snow gently off the lump, knows before he reveals the naked figure, the purple bruised ribs exposed to the elements, the mashed nose, the missing front teeth, the single leather glove on the man's left hand: the only piece of clothing he's wearing. Lloyd looks away, draws the searing cold through his nostrils, prepares himself for the inevitable, this time when he finds Jimmy Widman dead. The bile rises at the back of his throat, his pounding head pounds harder.

Lloyd exhales harshly, his breath hanging like a funeral shroud in the February air. He rolls Jimmy over onto his back, leans close to his mouth. He can't discern air or breath, warm-blooded animal or otherwise. And why is Jimmy naked? Doesn't make sense. If the Fleck boys have anything to do with that, he'll drive out to see them himself. Lloyd checks his radial pulse but can't find it. Jimmy's skin cold like the snow, like the ice floes that catch rootless boys' bodies in the North Saskatchewan River. Lloyd lays his ear on Jimmy's chest, catches a faint *thud thud thud*, irregular like arrhythmia beneath his ear. Hallelujah, hypothermia! It's the best Lloyd can hope for, the theory being you're not dead until you're warm and dead. Warm he can do.

Lloyd peels off his parka yet again, wraps Jimmy's freezing body in it. He runs back to the cruiser, radios in for an ambulance.

"We talking Widman?" the paramedic asks.

Lloyd hears the disdain in the man's voice.

"Animal, vegetable, or mineral?" asks the paramedic.

"Listen, we're not talking twenty questions, get off your goddamn butt and get down here."

"Yessir, Corporal Lloyd," the paramedic drawls like he's Texan.
Lloyd doesn't respond.

The radio rides static on the empty airwave. Lloyd radios Constable Pete in case the ambulance doesn't make it or gets conveniently sidetracked.

"What's up?" Lloyd asks.

"Helping Bill pull a stuck calf," Constable Pete says breathlessly.

"You at Bill's?"

"No, we're east of that on Crown land. Dang mother wandered off through the fence," says Constable Pete.

"How long you figure you'll be?"

"Another twenty on the calf, another forty back to town. You need me to come in now?" Constable Pete asks.

"No, I can manage, meet you back at the detachment."

Lloyd hangs the radio up, backs the cruiser as close as he can to where Jimmy is, opens the back-seat door. In the space of two minutes Jimmy's body has been completely covered in snow again. Lloyd brushes him off as best he can, drags Jimmy by the collar of his RCMP parka through the deepening snow to the cruiser. By the time he reaches the car, Lloyd's pushing a frigid sweat beneath his thin beige shirt. He lifts Jimmy into the car, slides him gently across the back seat, worried more about Jimmy's irregular heart than his broken ribs; that'll be the least of Jimmy's worries.

Wednesday, October 1987 » Lesa, age 31

A change of heart, a sudden presence of mind, not the aimless driving away from her mother's house in search of yet something else she doesn't need, Lesa pulls over to the payphone just beyond Airdrie. She deposits her coin in the silver slot, chants the memorized phone number, presses the metal buttons that are October cold to her touch. The phone rings on the other end. A woman's voice answers, not what Lesa expects, should she hang up?

"Good morning, Stewart and Green Barristers and Solicitors," the woman says.

Lesa pauses, doesn't know what to say.

"Hello?"

"I'm looking for a lawyer, I'm sorry, I've forgotten his name. He's tall, slim build, brown hair—" Lesa stops short of mentioning his boyish hands.

"That's Mr. Green. Please hold while I put you through."

Blue-suit man is Mr. Green. Lesa smiles. A large cattle truck rattles by on the highway, the whoosh of cold air up her back, the instant stench of manure in the air. She glimpses the blur of cattle inside, silent, morose as if they know what their destination is, first the feedlot, then the slaughterhouse. Despite the rank smell, the roar of the truck's engine sounds like applause/approval in her ears.

"Mr. Green speaking."

His voice is different than she anticipated, deeper, more businesslike. God, he sounds like a father, not hers, thank goodness, but someone's possibly. Then she realizes they hadn't exchanged so much as a single word between them during their carnal game of hide 'n' find at the airport.

"Mr. Goodtime Green?" Lesa says.

She hears him hesitate on the other end of the receiver.

He lets his breath out slowly.

"Would this be Storm?" he asks.

"Yes!"

She's surprised he knows who Storm is from the X-Men comic series that her boyfriend uses as wallpaper to cover over the crumbling plaster walls of his studio on Water Street. Now it's her turn to hesitate. She presses the phone into her ear over the sound of the traffic, the twisting wind, the swift thought of her boyfriend, her storm, her mind peeling away like the crush of cars on the highway, all bound for some place other than here.

"Nice to hear from you, Storm," Mr. Green says.

His voice loses the depth, the business, sounds soothing, washes over Lesa like a warm bath, glides over her whole body, makes her legs feel as if someone else will take charge, hold her up if only for a short while. She catches her knees from buckling. Speechless, she can't find the right words, any words.

God, she doesn't know how to do this. She wonders how her father did it? Surely a few uncut shots of tequila/rye/whisky would make this go down smoother. Seriously, how *do* people *do this straight*? She surmises that they don't. She pulls the solitary joint out of her Escher case, tries to light it, but the howling wind extinguishes her every lit match.

Mr. Green is silent on the other end, as if he knows she must come to this destination on her own accord, unlike the fettered cattle that don't have the luxury of choice, unlike her fettered mother.

"Mr. Green?"

"Storm?" he says evenly.

"Yes," says Lesa.

She knows what her destination is.

Wednesday, July 1961 » Jacqueline, age 27

After fried pork chops and mashed potatoes with mushroom soup gravy, Nate throws up on the Lego in the middle of the living room carpet. Jacqueline picks him up and runs him like a football down the hallway to the bathroom. His tiny face is flushed, a touch of hyperthermia.

"Too much sun, too much play, too much excitement." Jacqueline holds him over the toilet.

Someone has forgotten to flush and the water is murky and yellow, filled with too much toilet paper. Sylvie. Jacqueline flushes while Nate vomits into the roiling mess. The water and fresh bile rise to the rim of the toilet. Jacqueline feels her all-day morning sickness rise too. She's eighty-nine on the mother-Richter scale of zero to one hundred, and if the toilet bowl overflows Jacqueline will hit the hundred and fifty mark and then there will be no accounting for anything.

The acidy smell of Nate's vomit mixed with the too-rich odour of Campbell's mushroom soup makes Jacqueline feel like throwing up alongside Nate. She forces the bile back down her throat as the water in the toilet eddies and skirts the outer edge of the porcelain, then sucks down as quickly as it rose. Jacqueline lets out a deep, harsh breath.

In between vomiting, Nate lays across her lap and wonders why the policeman from next door spent so much time in the alley out behind their house and where was daddy? How come he wasn't the policeman that came?

"It's not safe in the alley for little children." Jacqueline strokes his red face. She doesn't mention his father's inconceivable absence. She is careful also not to mention the station wagon or Sylvie or why Lesa is holed up in her bedroom and didn't come out for dinner. Nate hangs his head over the edge of the toilet and vomits once more.

"There, there, little man," she says, pressing a cool washcloth to his forehead. She can hear Sylvie twisting the front door knob, but she knows Sylvie hasn't mastered it yet.

"Lesa," she hollers from the washroom. "Go see what Sylvie's doing."

Lesa comes out of her room and storms past the bathroom without even glancing at her mother.

Jacqueline sits on the floor holding Nate until he feels the need, then she steadies his shuddering body while he throws up.

"You'll feel better once you're done," she says, but she's not so sure.

Sylvie flits by the open bathroom door once, twice, five times from the living room to the end of the hall and back again.

"Lesa! Get Sylvie to sit down and play Lego," Jacqueline yells.

"There's throw-up on the Lego," Lesa yells back.

Yes, she'd forgotten. Throw-up on the Lego, on their turquoise carpet. Sylvie is running like a mad child around the house, Nate is sick with sunstroke. It's a hundred and five degrees in the locked house, her husband is missing in action, and Lesa is, well, she's defiant. And if it weren't for Nate's sickly, overheated face staring up into hers, flecks of mushroom on his chin and down the front of his T-shirt, then she'd simply get up and walk out of the house for good, for real this time, like Charles the cat from next door, like so many passing foster children.

Instead she fills the tub with lukewarm water and pours in a cap of bubble bath, which produces a see-through shade of army green. She gently tugs Nate's Superman shirt over his head, careful not to get vomit on him, then pulls off his Batman shorts and his Fantastic Four underwear and slides his small, hot body into the cool bath. For the moment, he's her superhero, her saviour.

Wednesday, February 1973 » Lloyd, age 40

Safely off the highway, and loaded in the back seat of Lloyd's cruiser, Jimmy lies near fatal in the fetal position. Lloyd has the heat cranked to hell and hot. Christ, it's a saving kind of day, not the usual sit, drive, sit, drink, sit some more, followed by too many late-night shots in Neville's lounge followed by too many early morning coffees in Neville's café.

Lloyd cracks the window in the cruiser open slightly to keep alert, awake in the hell-fire heat, his fatigue. There's no hospital in the town; he drives Jimmy to the doctor's house across the alley from his detachment. The veterinarian is next door. The doctor's waiting room and single treatment room for small emergencies are on the bottom floor of his three-storey house, the only walkout basement in the town. Seemingly extravagant where the rest of the town's houses are modest bungalows with giant yards, prosperous gardens in the summer that sustain them through these harsh winters north of Edmonton. Long cold months of protracted, uninterrupted miseries on the flat white prairies, snow up to your waist, perma-cold beneath your skin until spring comes, miraculously it seems. Then the hard snow melts, the ice flows in the North Saskatchewan River, the hardening around Lloyd's heart, and then, only then can he foresee himself doing his job for another year. He wipes his hand across his drawn face, glances into the back seat at Jimmy. No movement.

He backs the cruiser up to the doctor's door, leaves the car running while he gets out to find the waiting room door locked. Lloyd bounds up the front steps of the residence, rings the bell, but the doctor's wife, who acts as receptionist, triage nurse, and mother of four, isn't home either.

Damn, not much time here. He sprints across the alley to the veterinarian's house. The vet is in the middle of euthanizing a huge white animal the size of a small polar bear lying on the metal table. Its elderly owners are standing reverentially in the corner when Lloyd bursts in.

"Got a problem, hypothermia. Can you help?"

"Calf?" The vet doesn't look up.

"Man."

The vet glances over at the owners as he injects the last needle into the giant animal, a dog, a grand-something-or-other. A final twitch from the white dog on the table produces an audible sob from the white-haired woman in the corner. Her elderly husband puts his arm around her.

"I'm sorry," Lloyd offers.

"Is life," the elderly man says or asks, Lloyd doesn't know which.

The bald man wags his head as the vet tries to gently lift the dog off the table, but it's too large, too heavy. Lloyd takes the dog's gigantic head and the vet its rear. They engineer the dog into the next room while the elderly man and his wife scrutinize their every slip and near drop. The man leads his weeping wife out and they sit in their car watching as Lloyd scrambles back across the alley to his cruiser. He waits for them to depart. They don't, so Lloyd pulls the cruiser directly up on the frozen tundra beside them.

The vet comes out, and he and Lloyd carefully pull the inert body from the back of the cruiser. The elderly man rolls down his window.

"Is live?" he asks.

"That's the hope," Lloyd says, his breath heavy with the exertion of first the dog and now Jimmy. The man and woman remain in their car, watching as if at a drive-in movie. Lloyd gives them a sharp look. The bald man reverses the car, but then sits at the end of the driveway, the car idling great columns of carbon monoxide in the bitter air.

Once on the table, the vet strips off Lloyd's RCMP parka, the one glove. Tries Jimmy's radial artery, nothing. Listens with his stethoscope, then straightens up, nods at Lloyd. Faint pulse on the carotid. Goes into the back room where the large white dead dog is, comes out with an armload of blankets, which he wraps in layers around Jimmy's naked body.

"See any clothes along the way?" the vet asks.

"A regular breadcrumb trail on the highway," says Lloyd, baffled.

"Hypothermia fools its victims into thinking they're warm, hot like a Mexican beach," the vet says, filling the dog-grooming tub with lukewarm water.

"Christ almighty, who makes these things up?" Lloyd shakes his head, a freezing man discarding his clothes at minus twenty-two Fahrenheit, the north wind making it minus thirty?

"No rhyme," the vet says, tight-lipped.

After the tub is full, the vet peels the layers of blankets off until he reaches Jimmy's emaciated body curled inside like the caraway seed in a jawbreaker; Jimmy's jaw hangs implausibly.

"Dislocated," the vet says, gently testing the abnormal range of movement.

"Help me get him into this tub."

The vet lifts Jimmy by the shoulders, Lloyd takes his legs. Carefully they lower him into the tub, the vet laving the warm water over the core of Jimmy's body, stopping only to take his pulse, more laving, pulse, stethoscope to Jimmy's chest until he hears the regular, dull *thump-thump* of a functioning heart. He checks the carotid artery again, feels the blood chasing through Jimmy's veins. The vet reaches for a bottle of dog shampoo above the tub, tenderly washes Jimmy's matted hair, cleans the coagulated blood off his face, from his ears, takes a good look at his swollen eye.

"He'll live," the vet says. "But he's going to need some stitching up, some kind of aftercare. Any family?"

Lloyd shakes his head, thinks of Jimmy alone at his father's farmhouse with only wild turkeys for company. That won't do. He could drive him down to Edmonton General Hospital, but then they'd just release him after a week or two, and to whom? Where would Jimmy go? Spring still months shy this side of merciless February. No short-term solution is going to work for long-term Jimmy. He needs something more substantial.

Lloyd helps the vet take Jimmy out of the dog-grooming tub. They dry him off, wrap him in warm blankets that the vet has heated in the gas dryer. The colour back in Jimmy's mashed face, skeletal arms, legs, a few indecipherable words out of his mouth, not nearly the dead man Lloyd initially brought in, but warm *and* alive, a regular windfall.

"Can I leave him with you for a bit?" Lloyd asks. "I've got an errand to tend to."

The vet checks his animal roster in the black binder beneath the metal table. Flips through a couple pages, runs his finger down the lined page.

"He's good till 2:00, then I've got a feline op coming in."

Lloyd checks his watch, 11:27. If he hurries, he can catch Judge Wade before he leaves town.

"I'll send Constable Pete over to retrieve him; he can help you with the dog. See if you can track down the doctor, get him to take a look at that jaw of Jimmy's, his eye, see what he can do."

"Will do," the vet says, puts his hand on Jimmy's fetal, no longer fatal body, curled and undersized like a motherless calf on the metal table.

Lesa sits a quiet moment in her mother's car on the side of the highway, listening to the yowling wind as she exhales cigarette smoke out the open window, aware that she's smoking too much these days, will have to make a conscious effort to cut back once she returns home, but her stomach is jittery, her hands shaky. Should she call him back, call him off before it's too late? She doesn't know what she wants, just that she *wants* mindlessly to fill the hollows of herself. She considers again the precious and solitary joint she brought along but doesn't want to waste it too soon. Pre–Mr. Green? In-between Mr. Green? Post–Mr. Green? This is absurd; she doesn't even know his first name. Who sleeps mindlessly with Misters? She knows the answer to that. She stubs her John out in her mother's ashtray, pulls the joint out, lights it, takes three permissive drags, holding them in her lungs like for as long as she can bear, then breathes out slowly. The thick release of white smoke fills the air in her mother's car. She pinches the end off the joint with her bare fingertips, flicks it out the window, only just feels the burn, replaces the joint back in her silver case for later, for the disapproval on her brother's face, the hurt on her mother's, her already guilty conscience. She doesn't look at herself when she checks for traffic in the rear-view mirror, heads down the highway toward the next anonymous town on her map to nowhere.

» » »

She calculates the driving time from downtown Calgary to main-street Carstairs, roughly an hour, perhaps less given the motivated speed of Mr. Green. She parks her mother's car in front of Hunter's Country Kitchen (Mr. Green's suggestion), considers changing out of her Storm getup, then decides she likes the idea of her storm blowing into a town she doesn't know, likewise a town that doesn't know her. She could be anyone this Wednesday morning, so unlike herself, so unlike her faithful mother to her faithless father. In her pot-addled mind she's doing this for her mother, for all the loyal, needy/naive/trapped women out there.

Her edgy stomach reminds her that she's hungry, needs to be attended to before anything else gets in the way. She climbs out of the car, long Spandex legs, high-heeled boots, imagines herself a spokeswoman in a sports car ad, the promise of illicit things related to neither cars nor sports. The fall air feels charged around her, *sex, sex, sex* flashing phosphorous orange, neon in her mind like the XXX Video store down the street from her apartment in Vancouver's West End. Hardly the good feminist she envisions herself to be. Or the only good one, like the stunning lesbian at Emily Carr, whose feminist offence was to dress to kill, if only to torment the males that couldn't have her. Funny. Lesa can't make the distinction at the moment, good or bad; her stomach and charged groin won't let her.

She walks down the street in search of a 7-Eleven or a Mac's, any place she might pick up a bag of something salty. Two laps around the sleepy town and no fast answers in sight, she peers inside the steamy windows of Hunter's Country Kitchen. She wonders why Mr. Green chose this place? Most likely the choices are minimal in a prairie town with the population base of a movie theatre. Or perhaps this is standard procedure for him? She doesn't like the thought of that, prefers to think she's unique, special. She goes inside. The $3.99 breakfast special doodled on a white board reads: Keep on the Sunny Side (with accompanying happy face), ham (loosely drawn pig), home-fires (misspelled), farm eggs (pair of amorous chickens, smiling), coffee. Four beefy men, who smell like the cattle they apparently work with, are seated at the front counter eating smiling eggs and fried pig. They pause to stare at her as she stands at the front door, waits for the lone waitress in the restaurant to seat her. The waitress waves her over to the empty booths.

Under different circumstances she could bring herself to face the men dead on, smile bravely beneath her brown freckles, but the pot conspires to make her shy, less confident, paranoid even. She doesn't know why she bothers with it. Stopping just short of swivelling completely on their red tattered stools, the men eyeball her sidelong in her tight black Spandex, the stiletto-ness of her pleather boots, the unconscious cape she wears for her mother. She avoids their watchful eyes, and for the fourteen backward feminist seconds, the time it takes her to traverse the small restaurant, her skin jumps, crawls, bucks uncertainly beneath her storm.

She sinks down into the dilapidated leather booth, cigarette burns, minute slashes, the larger gashes patched over with ordinary grey duct tape that sticks to her Spandex as she slides across the seat. Hardly the swank restaurant, the heady chalice of expensive red wine she imagined, waiting on a man with boyish hands whose first name she doesn't know. She can't quell the tremor up and down her body, can't fully decide which way to fall. Stay or go? She looks up tentatively at the four men, catches them staring at her. They nod, smile politely beneath curled moustaches, heavy brows, John Deere ball caps, go back to their coffee and home-fires.

The waitress plonks a handwritten menu down on the table; the host of greasy fingerprints make it almost illegible. The waitress splashes black, burnt-smelling coffee in Lesa's white cup, shifts from one ample hip to the other and back again while Lesa peruses the menu.

"Whaddya have, honey?" she asks.

"The special, please," Lesa says.

"Whaddya have on there?" the waitress asks, pointing at her costume with the end of her chewed-up Bic pen.

"Storm?" Lesa tries.

The waitress shakes her head.

"Don't know it. How do you want your eggs?"

"On the sunny side," Lesa says, tries to suppress the stoned, ironic grin creeping onto her face.

"White or brown toast?"

"Brown," Lesa answers.

"Bacon, ham, or sausage?"

"Bacon, crisp."

"Hash browns or home fries?"

"Home-fires."

The waitress busy with her order pad doesn't respond.

"Cream?"

"Black."

"Those are some nice black boots," the waitress says, admiring them momentarily before she picks up the menu, goes back to the counter, and pours a round of five-cent refills for the four men. Lesa can hear the waitress explaining, "Some storm from somewhere, who the hell knows?"

Lesa sips on the burnt coffee, looks around the rundown restaurant at the fake wood panelling identical to what her mother had in their basement in the late 1970s. The supposed good years, the heyday, when she and Nate had moved out, seeking their own places. Nate across the country in Ottawa, Lesa in Vancouver. Teenage Clare technically still at home but hardly there. When money and time opened up after all those difficult, intense years for her mother raising children, followed by a decade of caregiving for her father, who by then was bruised, yellow-skinned, terminal, sitting faithfully in his La-Z-Boy chair smoking thick, odorous cigars. Her mother went on aging two-fold while her father died too young. And here now in 1987, the good years long past, her father gone, her mother alone, Clare moved out, the fake wood panelling in their basement hasn't changed one iota; atonement, it seems, for no one.

Lesa's muddled mind runs the gamut: her sculptor boyfriend pre-occupied with steak dresses and burnt toast, her lonely mother, her faithless/fateful father, and now this morning Mr. Green at the air-port, like a soft, shimmery thing out of nowhere, someone who cares. Or so she hopes. She imagines his kind eyes resting on her flushed face, can feel the sure-man touch of his boyish hands, one swift, single moment, repealing not only her mind-numbing presence, but also the irretrievable future. What then? What of her boyfriend? Her mother? Dead father, disappointed brother? Reversible/irreversible? She looks up from her reverie, sees the men from the front counter watching her with renewed interest. Does her face tell what her mind is revealing at this moment? She hopes not.

The waitress sets the platter of crisp bacon and greasy eggs and home-fires down, pours more black coffee into her cup. Lesa dives in, glad for the diversion, surprised by her sudden need to hurry, her overwhelming hunger, her wavering mind clearing, solidifying with each bite, each gulp, hardly a stray thought as she devours her Keep on the Sunny Side breakfast special.

She takes a last sobering slug of coffee, leaves a ten-dollar bill on the table for the five-dollar tab. The waitress picks it up.

"Need change, honey?" she asks.

"Not from you," Lesa says.

Lesa unsticks her Spandex from the duct tape as she slides across the superficial gashes on the booth seat. She doesn't need to know Mr. Green's first name. It doesn't matter; what matters is that she gets the heck out of Dodge before he appears and then everything goes sideways, stormy, irreversible, irretrievable.

Time yet, she thinks, the time her father didn't get. She's doing this for him.

"Bless you, darling, have a good day," the waitress hollers across the restaurant. The four men nod. Good God, she's trying.

It's 8:30 PM. No word from her husband. How is that possible? Jacqueline is exhausted. Her head is woozy. She realizes all she's eaten today is Sylvie's leftover Spam and cheese sandwich from early this morning. From then on it's been a steady flow of Peter Jackson, the man she should have ordered, and black coffee. Likely the heat and lack of food and Jacqueline's nausea are the cause of her light-headedness, and because of it, she allows herself a treacherous game of *what if*? *What if* she hadn't gone to get coffee for her neighbour at precisely that moment? *What if* that man had managed to pull Sylvie into the car? *What if* her husband doesn't come home tonight? *What if* this unrelenting nausea means another Sylvie? Oh, God, she can't think about that. Her hands shake uncontrollably as she picks up Lego from the carpet covered in Nate's sticky vomit.

"Two more hours," she says out loud to herself, to Nate, who is sprawled out on his back on their tattered black and red tartan sofa in a fresh white T-shirt and Superman underwear, asleep. Exhausted after the vomiting, his bath. Two more hours, then perhaps when the late July sun goes down, then so will Sylvie, who is safely at the kitchen table right now filling her sheet of blue-lined paper row by row, line after line with minute circles in circles that she draws with a ballpoint pen until the entire sheet is full on both sides. It's one of the few things Sylvie can sit still for, on a good day sometimes for two hours. At least she's not sprinting about the house. Jacqueline lets her be.

Lesa is in her room. She came out long enough to occupy Sylvie while Nate was vomiting, long enough to slather a piece of Wonder Bread with peanut butter and then disappear back into her room. But not before Jacqueline retrieved the two glass doorknobs and screwed them securely into place so Lesa could neither lock herself in nor her mother out, whatever the intent.

Jacqueline looks up from the sticky-sick Lego and on the muted television sees Ethel and Lucy dressed in factory clothes at a conveyor belt, wrapping the candy as it comes down the line, then as the conveyor belt speeds up, Lucy and Ethel stuffing chocolates in their mouths, their hats, down their shirts. Despite her fatigue or because of it, Jacqueline laughs until her eyes water. Coincidentally, it's also Lesa's favourite show. Jacqueline wonders if she and Lesa are more alike than she realizes. She goes down the hall to tell Lesa that while she doesn't normally get to watch *I Love Lucy* because it's past her bedtime, as a special treat, she can tonight. Lesa is lying sideways on her bed, still dressed in her plaid skort and pink-frilled blouse from this morning. The heat less so now, but still warm and ominously close, like before a thunderstorm. She's staring up at the swirl plaster ceiling.

"Lesa?"

She doesn't answer.

"*You Love Lucy* is on if you'd like to watch it," Jacqueline says, smiling at Lesa.

Jacqueline walks across the room and sits on the edge of the bed. She puts her hand on Lesa's back. Lesa doesn't move.

"Lesa, Mommy is not mad at you," she says, meaning to explain this afternoon, Sylvie, the officer, although the stiffness in her voice contradicts her. And there is no denying the sudden fury building unreasonably, coursing through her at this moment. Why does she feel this way? Lesa sits up and looks at her keenly. Jacqueline knows the ball is in her court. Of course it is, she's the adult here, but she can't read Lesa's lightly freckled face. Accusing? Forgiving? Or is it beyond-her-age understanding? She doesn't know. Lesa's strawberry-blond hair is fine but messy, so very different than Sylvie's flawless black glimmering hair, as if God intended that to make up for the rest of it. Jacqueline would like to reach out and smooth down the perpetual rat's nest at the back, and hold Lesa and tell her she loves her, but she's afraid to. Jacqueline knows the brink; she's been there before. Once, she couldn't calm Sylvie, who was shrieking uncontrollably in her crib. She shook her twice, three times, then the realization hit her that this was where a mother ceased to be a mother and became something else instead—an unintentional monster. She removes her hand from Lesa's back as if she's on fire. Lesa can't, won't understand, Jacqueline thinks. Lesa's unwavering green eyes hold her gaze, waiting for her to be a mother instead of the monster she feels growing inside.

Jacqueline stands up abruptly and leaves the room without saying a word. She locks herself in the washroom. The faint smell of vomit still in the air. She ignores the mushroom gravy spewed over the toilet and the blue bathmat and closes the cracked lid and sits on it, smokes a cigarette, smoothing out her serrated edges, until the *dis*-ease takes over once more and flatlines her into the null and void.

In the living room Jacqueline leaves the television on even though *I Love Lucy* has already ended and Lesa didn't come out. Jacqueline thinks about going to check on her, but then thinks it may be better to let sleeping monsters lie. They can discuss it in the morning when everyone feels better.

After she's done picking up the Lego and scrubbing the spray of vomit as best she can from the turquoise carpet, Jacqueline looks over at sleeping Nate. She'd forgotten about him. She looks at his gangly, sun-browned limbs splayed out in complete and utter abandonment as only children can do. She resists the urge to go over and bundle him up in her arms and nuzzle his skinny neck that looks as if it can't possibly support his toddler-large head but does. She knows eventually his body will grow into it. But for now, all she wants to do is tuck her children safely beneath her arms and keep them there forever, if that's what it takes. She covers Nate lightly with a clean bath towel. She'll put him to bed shortly, and hopefully Lesa will be asleep too.

She carries the bin of Lego down the hall to the bathroom. She peers into the kitchen to see that yes, Sylvie is at the kitchen table, her chicken-wing shoulder blades jut out, mere skin over bone as she hunkers over her drawing, absolutely absorbed in the moment. Jacqueline pauses, mesmerized by the extraordinary power of focus and stillness that Sylvie finds only in drawing. And Jacqueline imagines beyond Sylvie's scarred lips and crooked dark eyes that *if* Sylvie were normal, she *could* grow, as Nate will into his head. But in a less tangible way for Sylvie. In a way that includes a future, what every mother wishes for her children: chance, choice, possibility. Perhaps Sylvie could build a serene life as an artist, instead of this trapped, frenetic existence: all crossed wires and misfiring neurons. Jacqueline tiptoes across the linoleum, careful not to disturb Sylvie from her reverie, and peers over her shoulder: an entire sheet of meticulous rows of faultless blue circles. Jacqueline doesn't know whether to laugh or cry.

Lloyd drives swiftly through the town to the small brick courthouse. Stationary smoke from the metal stacks hangs like exclamation marks above Neville's! Eve's! the hardware store! Hardly a soul on the cold street as Lloyd takes the courthouse steps two at a time. Staffing the front desk is Doris Michelchuk, former town council, egg farmer, hair the colour of a chocolate soufflé teased up high like a country singer. Corporal Lloyd waits until she stops typing.

"Judge Wade around?" he asks.

Doris goes through the pretense of checking the day's Rota. Doris is adept at knowing precisely where everyone in the town is at any given moment of the day, but she checks anyway.

"Nope," she says, closing the book. "He's not here at the moment."

"A little under the weather, corporal?" she asks.

"All in today, Doris."

Doris shakes her brown unmoving mass, purses her orange lips.

"He stepped out," says Doris.

Lloyd waits. Doris goes back to clattering on her Smith Corona.

"Heemno," she says under her breath.

Lloyd smiles. Ukrainian for *shit*.

She stops typing.

"He's over at Neville's," she says.

"You're a prize, Doris," says Lloyd, winking at her.

Doris pulls a bottle of correction fluid from the desk drawer.

"You're welcome," she says, watching Corporal Lloyd exit the building and jog across the street to Neville's, leaving his cruiser parked out front of the courthouse.

Neville's lounge smells musty: dank, festering yeast. The bar dark in the middle of the day, so the patrons don't have to be reminded that this is also the middle of the week. When they should be at work instead of killing the daylight hours in a darkened lounge sitting around beer-soaked terry-cloth tables—the festering decay of Wednesday. Lloyd squints into the dim room, finds Judge Wade holding court in the back along with a couple of the paramedics, no doubt the smartass on the radio earlier who never showed up, the night security guard who speaks mostly Ukrainian, fractured English. Lloyd hires the security guard whenever he has a special guest in his holding cell—not the infrequent townsfolk gone off on the occasional funk. But *special*, like the guy they picked up for a broken tail light on his Chevy truck. Corporal Lloyd and Constable Pete not impressed when they had to chase the bastard over three miles of farmers' field, through a swamp, and then into a prairie slough for a broken tail light? Even less impressed after Constable Pete tackled him, and Corporal Lloyd cuffed the man's hands behind his back, and they took him back to the detachment. The three of them covered in sheep shit and quagmire from head to Strathcona boot to find out the guy was wanted on a Canada-wide warrant for killing his entire family. That kind of special.

Lloyd walks over to the table, ignores the paramedics, turns his attention to Judge Wade: fat slab of a man, a large heart of silver quarters that he doles out to Lloyd's kids like a Vegas slot machine every time Lloyd throws a poker party in the concrete basement of his house. Judge Wade is the real thing. Genuinely cares through thick and thin, cases that make you cringe, and worse, the cases you couldn't make up that make your head reel, your stomach sick, make that first shot of Bacardi's, Crown Royal, Glenfiddich, and the taste of strange women, sweet and necessary; to everyone their niche. The judge's niche: Southern Comfort in Lloyd's northern town.

Corporal Lloyd takes off his RCMP parka, and the cardamom scent of baby, the Wild Turkey reek of Jimmy lingers in the dank air, poles apart, but innocent all the same. He hangs the parka on the back of the chair across the aisle, orders two Comforts. The judge finishes his drink, nods at the paramedics, slides out of his chair, joins Corporal Lloyd at his table. Lloyd checks his watch—11:55, technically morning still—he raises his glass.

"Dobroho rankoo," Lloyd says.

"Yes, a good morning," Judge Wade says, his case heard, done, adjourned already. The judge jangles the ice in his glass; the two of them knock it back in one toss. Lloyd feels the velvet liquid burn smooth down the back of his throat; smooth the hair of last night's dog. Seventeen hours into his twelve-hour shift, the fatigue hits him like a narcotic; Lloyd's muscles relax into the Southern Comfort.

"What can I do you for?" Judge Wade flags down the waitress, orders a couple more. Lloyd wipes his palm over his tired face.

"Coffee," Lloyd says to the waitress.

"Dead on my feet," he says to the judge.

"Long night?" the judge asks.

"Longer Wednesday and not done yet."

"What do you need?"

"A court order for Jimmy."

"Wildman?"

"Widman," Lloyd says. "Jimmy Widman."

Jimmy's been up in front of the judge's bench, mostly mild misdemeanours involving vagrancy, public drunkenness, urinating on a government building—specifically, Doris Michelchuk's court-house—he's no stranger to Judge Wade.

"What's the order for?" Judge Wade asks.

"For Ponoka, Michener, doesn't matter. I need him declared incompetent, incapacitated, whatever the legal term is."

The waitress sets the drinks down, Lloyd's coffee. Lloyd watches the judge savour his Comfort, then Lloyd pours his into the coffee, two for the price of one.

"Not that simple, Lloyd. He needs to be referred by a GP, then assessed by regional health, interviewed by not one, but two psychiatrists, then . . ."

"He needs a way out, judge. He'll be dead before anyone gets to him."

The judge looks him in the eye.

"Fleck boys?"

Lloyd nods.

"What's that stuff Widman drinks? Wild spirit, Kentucky turkey? Hundred-and-one proof? Serious heemno—that'll kill anyone."

Lloyd shakes and nods his head at the same time, agreement and disagreement on his weary face.

95

"He's got other things going on, Wade."

He's watching the judge, but he's thinking Sylvie, the unfinished matter of Sylvie.

Judge Wade pauses, orders another Comfort from the passing waitress. Lloyd waves her off.

"Bring me a fresh napkin," the judge says to the waitress.

Judge Wade offers him a cigar. The two smoke in silence. Lloyd looks around the dark room, the coffee and Comfort enough to give him a lukewarm buzz, but not enough to transport him out of the mounting discomfort he feels deep in his intestines. Doesn't matter which way Judge Wade falls; it's all dread or dead. He puffs on his cigar while the judge scribbles something on the fresh napkin.

Wednesday, October 1987 » Lesa, age 31

Having left Carstairs, gotten the heck out of Dodge in the hurry that she's in, Lesa's got an urgent, pressing purpose on her mind that she didn't know she had prior to this morning. Sylvie. She fumbles for a cigarette from her silver case. She'll save the half-joint for later when she really needs it, when she pulls up once more in front of her mother's house, something she's not looking forward to. The car lighter pops out, Lesa lights her John, realizes she's no player, never was. She can't really believe she went as far as she did. Not that the idea hadn't occurred to her before, the pure exhilaration of an appealing stranger. At times the inclination to simply let go, let fly, is stronger than she is, exaggerated now by her father's death. Life is short. But she's certainly never acted on the impulse. The near miss with Mr. Green makes Lesa doubt her ability to fly straight. She's got to stop this moving away from things: herself, her estranged mother, the memory of her dead father, her distant boyfriend. She needs to find something to move toward.

She's driving too fast to notice the animal running across the six-lane highway playing Frogger with the slow-moving John

Deere tractor, the duelling semi trucks hauling Safeway and Co-op fighting for supremacy in the fast lane, two ordinary citizens in nondescript cars, the farmer in a Ford pickup and the front grill of her mother's Toyota.

Lesa catches the mottled grey-brown thing out of the corner of her eye too late. She broadsides the animal in broad daylight. The animal bounces off the front of the car so that Lesa sees the coyote slowed in the space of time that feels like the prairies themselves: wide, open, expansive, but is actually a mere second split into one hundredths. The animal's ochre coat is the same colour as the surrounding flatlands, the dead wheat. She sees the coyote's eyes go wide, dark suddenly, out of the blue into the blue of the anything-can-happen prairie sky. The aberrant U-curve of its body as it arcs heavenbound makes Lesa feel sick in the pit of her belly. She slams on the brakes. The maroon New Yorker that has been riding her ass for the last ten kilometres fishtails around (God, please don't let it be Mr. Green), narrowly clears her back bumper, then runs so close alongside she could reach out and touch him, like a long-distance phone commercial, were she the passenger of this vehicle and not the hazardous driver.

In the rapid space of a single heartbeat, Lesa loses her cigarette, stops breathing, afraid that if she so much as glances away, then the two cars will become one, another Highway 2 North headline in tomorrow's newspaper. Deadline. She's not interested in dying. She maintains her steely grip on the steering wheel, steals a glance at the driver (thank you, God, not Mr. Green), his eyes the same as hers, the coyote's—harshly attentive, wide awake to the potential precursor of their own wakes. The man doesn't take his eyes off her, that acute recognition of the erratic line between life and/or their next breath.

The New Yorker drifts impossibly past. The driver slides in front of her, brakes hard as if she's only playing at this! A terrifying game of alpha driver at the giddying speed of one hundred and forty kicks/clicks an hour. Surely he saw the flying coyote? Lesa stands on her brakes so as not to hit him. The driver's middle finger pointing *not* up but horizontally out his open window. Lesa understands the double sexual affront of his gesture.

She pulls the car over to the side of the highway, shuts the ignition off, glances into the rear-view mirror. No other cars in sight. No in-flight coyote either. Her heart beats rabid, canine. The polyester plastic smell of burning velour alerts her to the lost cigarette in the back seat of the car. She stretches back, can't quite reach the smouldering butt, so climbs over the console to the passenger seat, but still can't manage; her hands, her breath, her heart are erratic, trembling with wasted adrenalin. She pushes the passenger door open intending to access the burning cigarette from the back seat, steps out onto the side of the road, the sharp stilettos of her super boots dig deep into the soft shoulder, throwing her off kilter.

She wavers uncertainly; her widespread arms floundering like a marooned angel in that loose chasm between heaven and hell, the ability to right herself, or pitch headlong down the steep embankment? Lesa sucks in the lingering exhaust from her mother's car as Murphy's law kicks in. She pitches headlong into the deep ditch, executing a flawless somersault not unlike the side rolls she learned on the Smoky Lake girls' volleyball team in 1973. The year she turned seventeen. The year the perversity of the universe kicked in. The year her father was diagnosed with multiple myeloma.

Lesa rolls helplessly to the bottom of the ditch, her fire-retardant cape wrapping her arms round her body tight, like she's been straitjacketed.

"Fuck," she yells to no one in particular, fights to free her arms, lies in the deep trough breathing shallowly, staring up at the razor-blue sharp of the sky above, her whole body quaking. She feels suddenly foolish for: her foul mouth, her Storm getup, her straitjacket cape—ironic, she thinks, given that she's headed up to Michener—her expert roll, Mr. Green. The blond stubble of last season's wheat pierces her skin like infinitesimal arrows, like Saint Francis or Saint Sebastian—one of them God's glorious guardian of birds, animals, the environment—the other poor bastard shot full of arrows. She doesn't know which one to be. She lies in the midst of highway litter, discarded Coke and beer cans, and cigarette butts, her cigarette alight in the back seat of her mother's car.

Sitting up brusquely in the trough, Lesa shakes her head to clear the no-see-em flies she sees, then spots the grounded coyote not two metres away in the same sad trench.

The animal is inert, motionless, dark blood pooling around its mouth, possibly from its torso. She doesn't like the angle of the coyote's spine either. It's dead. Of course it's dead. What did she think? That you could broadside an animal at that speed and have the animal lope miraculously off into the woods to heal itself?

Her eyes well up. She's killed a living thing. Makes her think, illogically ill timed, of her saltwater fish, her prized Clown and Puffer that jumped ship and/or aquarium in her Vancouver apartment. Why? she thought at the time. Why would they do that? They had real curling plankton, authentic seaweed imported from the Philippines waving in the gentle current of their carefully filtered water. Bubbling mermaids and sunken ships with likelife barnacles, Sweetlips and Triggers and Groupers et al., a one-foot spotted Eel. Even so, the two fish jumped, thinking perhaps that the glass or water was greener on the other side. She found them behind the tank when one of her three illegal (they live in a pet-free apartment zone) miniature Dobermans was nosing around; the Clown and the Puffer dehydrated, not necessarily respiring, but not dead yet either.

She couldn't tell in the initial hysteria of discovery, so she put them in a gold transparent mixing bowl filled with salt water she retrieved from the tank. Not wanting to put them straight into the tank itself, in case cannibalism set in the other fish. She never could come to terms with the primordial nature of nature. She set them by the kitchen window, barely able to force herself out the door to the casino on Davie Street. Hoping that when she came home at 3:00 or 4:00 AM after a long meaningless night of pit-bossing, she'd find not only her sculptor boyfriend present for a change instead of at his art studio, but the fish miraculously revived from their misplaced adventure.

She found neither.

She sits in the present tense in the ditch, watches the lifeless coyote all blurry and watery in her vision. Can't stop herself from thinking about all the other living things she has inadvertently killed: the black squirrel that landed with a definitive death thud at her feet, that her ankle-height Dobermans tore limb from limb fighting over the unfortunate rodent. Or the neighbourhood canine she nicked while shortcut-alley driving too fast in Vancouver, but the dog lived anyway. Lesa sees it from time to time, the dog's unwieldy three-legged hobble along the front side of the street. Neither one of them frequents the back lane anymore.

She can't quite believe this holey kismet-knit sweater is hers. She's such a lover of animals, of life in general. Surely the kindred spirit of Saint Francis? She's done this through her rushing about, her own rash stupidity, never taking the time to think things through, her reckless, high-wire ways. And here again speeding down the highway this morning like a maniacal woman desperate for redemption from the past, the present tension between her mother/lover/sister/brother. Her uncertain future rolled all into one garbage-filled trough on the side of Highway 2 with a dead coyote in it.

Wednesday, July 1961 » Jacqueline, age 27

The doorbell rings at 10:45 PM. It's not her husband who some-times misplaces his keys, nor is it the kind constable from next door, but his wife, Mary-Lynn. Jacqueline does a cursory glance at the state of her living room before she opens the door. She's tucked a peach-coloured bath towel around Nate, who is slumbering heavily, snoring lightly on the chesterfield; the broken wicker basket full of newly dirtied clothes, the splash of vomit on the carpet almost dry and only faintly odorous. The washed Lego spread out across the bookshelf and on top of the muted television drying. She opens the door.

"Come in," Jacqueline whispers.

"I've come to see if everything is all right, I heard your hus-band—" Mary-Lynn says.

She doesn't make a move to enter the house. She sees sleeping Nate.

"Isn't home." Jacqueline finishes the sentence for her.

From the flush on Mary-Lynn's normally pale face, Jacqueline knows that her husband's truancy is now public information, and by tomorrow will be all over the neighbourhood. She can't stand the idea of every wife on the block indignant on her behalf, she imagines, because who could side with her husband in such a case? No, it's not on her behalf she truly cares about, but the children's. Her husband wasn't there for his children, and that betrayal is far worse than any woman he may have slept with. The chickadees, two-note refrain of *Be-there* where her husband is concerned died a long time ago, years before this afternoon. In truth his presence fades with each child they have. She can't think about the swirling baby in her uterus, it makes her anxious, nauseated.

"Thank you for your help this afternoon with Nate and Lesa," Jacqueline says to steer the conversation away from her husband.

She knows she should be used to his absence by now, like half the other RCMP wives on the block, Mary-Lynn as well, but she's not. She's twenty-seven, young enough to still want her husband despite his duplicity. And there are times in this life that simply you need someone.

"It's the least I could do, considering," Mary-Lynn says and looks down the quiet, dark street at a flash of lightning.

Does she know about the reckless hug? Jacqueline wonders. Did her husband tell her that too? No, she will not feel shame for that—it was need, honest-to-God, down-on-your-knees need. Regardless, her face burns. She can't look Mary-Lynn in the eye.

She's enormously thankful for Mary-Lynn, who ran through the neighbourhood this afternoon after the man in the station wagon sped away, gathering Nate and Lesa for her, alerting the other mothers. Jacqueline is also acutely aware that none of the mothers came over afterward, nor called. And tomorrow when news of her absent husband reaches them, if they offer nothing, not sympathy, not indignation, then she will be fine. It's what she expects anyway.

Mary-Lynn stands stiffly in the doorway.

"Are you sure you won't come in?" Jacqueline asks.

She knows Mary-Lynn means well, in spite of her standoffish nature. Otherwise why else would Mary-Lynn be here at 10:45 at night? Notwithstanding, she has to admit, it's a little like receiving solace from the Queen, distant and cold, however well intended. Besides, she doesn't want pity from her or any of the other mothers in the neighbourhood. She wants to put Sylvie, who is still wandering about the house, to bed and sleep for twenty-four hours straight in the hope that when she wakes up, this will all be a remote memory, a faded nightmare.

"I don't want to wake your children, it's late. I wanted to make sure you were all right," Mary-Lynn says and turns to go down the steps.

At the bottom, she pauses and looks back at Jacqueline.

"God looks after us all," she says, and when Jacqueline fails to respond, "Are you sure you're all right?"

"I'm tired," says Jacqueline, "so God-forsaken tired."

Jacqueline feels the metal burrs she collects beneath her skin so her children won't have to.

Wednesday, February 1973 » Lloyd, age 40

Lloyd's the first to spot Constable Pete as he bursts into Neville's lounge, standing a moment at the front door to adjust his vision to the darkened room.

"Over here, constable," Lloyd says. The paramedics, the waitress, the bartender, the security guard, several other patrons pause briefly to stare at Constable Pete, then go back to the important business of imbibing and selling.

Pete sprints across the room. He's out of breath, covered in snow and cow shit, straw and calf blood, reeks to some low manger.

"Jesus, Saint Peter, you could have cleaned up a little." Lloyd waves his cigar in the air to cover the stench of heemno.

Judge Wade smiles, doesn't offer the constable a seat. Constable Pete stands uncomfortably in front of them. He's bursting with something.

"Well, Pete, what is it?" Corporal Lloyd asks.

Pete can't speak for breathing.

"I ran over," he says. "Didn't want the inspector to see the car here."

He tries to catch his breath; it's a full twelve country blocks from the detachment to Neville's in the frigid cold.

"Inspector?" Lloyd cocks his ear to one side, his face paling despite the full bloom of Southern Comfort.

Yes, he's off duty but in full uniform in a licensed lounge. Good thing he left the cruiser parked at the courthouse, an unplanned alibi, if it comes to that.

"He got wind, I don't know how—but he knows. He's on his way over here now."

Lloyd stands up, light-headed, almost falls back into his chair, stops to butt his cigar out in the overflowing ashtray.

"No, go, get out." Constable Pete motions toward the back door of the lounge.

"Shchastluvo," the judge says, hands him the napkin.

Lloyd tips his hat at the judge. He's going to need all the good Ukrainian luck he can find. He stuffs the napkin sight unseen into the breast pocket of his beige shirt.

Corporal Lloyd and Constable Pete leave through the back door. The inspector from Edmonton enters through the front door.

Judge Wade waves him over, impervious.

"Seen Corporal Lloyd?" The inspector asks, dense black brows knotted on his porpoise-broad forehead.

Judge Wade gestures in the thick air, puffs on his cigar.

"Not today," the judge says.

The inspector's mouth is set in a straight lip as he surveys the patrons of the lounge, the RCMP parka on the back of the chair across from the judge, the still-burning cigar in the ashtray. Judge Wade watches him through half-closed eyes, sips his Southern Comfort. He's got nothing to worry about; more power than an inspector, and they both know it. The inspector doesn't bother saying goodbye.

Wednesday, October 1987 » Lesa, age 31

In the trench, Lesa thinks she sees the animal's soul rising like discernible vapours, like a watery wake of smoke from its inert body, heavenbound for good, for great, for God this time. She lets out a final sob, takes a deep breath, regains herself, looks up at the wide blue sky, finds an undersized comfort, like too-small underwear, but consoling nonetheless.

She digs around her Spandex body for a tissue, finds a slightly used Air Canada napkin tucked into the top of her boots, wipes the salt water leaking from her eyes, down her cheeks, her chin, her neck. She glances over at the dead animal, realizes in horror/ joy that the animal's chest is heaving. The thing is still alive! The coyote is alive! She jumps to her feet, unsteady in the wake of everything, dances around the ditch. She checks her non-existent pockets again for something to stop the bleeding. Comes up with nothing. She fumbles with the knotted string at her throat, instead rips it off, and holds the black cape out like the Grim Reaper's toreador.

The animal's chest is labouring heavily, plainly, she doesn't know how she missed that before. And the troubling pool of black blood around the coyote's mouth is spreading, but its dark eye is alive, glittering with the life she and Saint Francis hold so dear. Oh, she's sure, she's so sure she can save it. She's elated at this second chance. The idea of darning the hole in her thin kismet. She stops dancing, crouches down on her hands and knees so as not to terrify the poor animal. But then as she moves closer, the coyote bares its awful yellow sharp(!) teeth and snarls. She stands up abruptly, alpha woman. The animal watches wildly through one eye, tries to drag its chest-labouring shattered body away from her. Oh God, she thinks, not that. She can't be yet the second coming of the coyote's demise. She puts her hand out as if to stop the animal or perhaps herself, but the coyote struggles back anyway, leaving the slick dark trail of its leaky blood over the blond stubble wheat. Each drag pierces her body.

Maintaining a safe distance from the coyote, she averts her eyes, so as not to appear confrontational; wonders if she should run up and find another pay phone, call Mr. Green at his office? Would he be back yet? She glances at her watch, 10:30 AM. He's likely not back. Not really an option given the circumstances of her sudden disappearance. Perhaps she could flag down a truck driver on the highway, get him to radio a veterinarian. Although she doesn't know what vet would come out to fight a flea-infested coyote for its life. Fish and Game possibly, but she knows in her animal heart that the solution would be a single gunshot wound to the head, not the reassurance of a fire-retardant cape belonging to a super woman. She looks down the ditch at the kilometres of garbage, everything, including herself, the waning coyote, covered in grey highway grit from the passing cars above.

She realizes there is nothing to be done, flimsy kismet and knitted sweaters alike. All she can do in this definitive moment, which has nothing to do with God is good or God is great, let us thank him for our food, but everything earthly, human: morass, muck and thorny crowns. All she can do is act as witness. Carry out the animal's rightful wake, watch it draw its last secular breath. She gazes up at the wild blue sky, a white cloud congealing on the distant horizon. She looks back at the coyote, but all she sees is her mother in the front seat of her father's Plymouth Fury, something in her arms, a lethal white cloud solidifying in a closed car. Lesa powerless to stop it.

Wednesday, July 1961 » Jacqueline, age 27

Sheets of white light flash across the dark horizon for a split second, followed by the distant reverberation of thunder. A summer storm is brewing. Jacqueline is grateful; the humidity in the house is unbearable, though thunder makes her uneasy. She counts after each flash: one, two, three, four seconds waiting for the disquieting *crack* like a leather whip as she sits on their split toilet lid, smoking, watching Sylvie play in the tub.

"Keep the water in the tub, Sylvie," she says every minute or so, regardless of what Sylvie is doing, to remind her not to raise both her arms then drop them like rag doll limbs into the water. Sylvie looks at her curiously, and then goes back to plummeting Lesa's Barbie that Sylvie cut all the hair off of last week into the cloud of white bubbles. She puts her arms over her head.

"Arms down, Sylvie."

Sylvie looks at her again, startled, as if she just realizes Jacqueline is there.

Jacqueline shakes her head. Sylvie puts her arms down.

"Let's get you to bed. It's almost midnight. Mommy wash your hair?" Jacqueline says. Sylvie loves getting her hair washed. It's one of three things, along with Smarties and drawing, that Sylvie can be still through.

Jacqueline folds a towel beside the tub and gets down on her knees.

"Lay back, Sylvie. Mommy will hold your head."

Sylvie stretches out freely, trusting herself wholly to Jacqueline, who cradles her head in her hands. Sylvie moves her small, sinewy body back and forth, agile like a snake as she floats on the surface of the water; lucent ripples radiate out from her, lap against the side of the tub, spill over.

"Be still, Sylvie."

But Sylvie can't hear her; she's in her own faraway world.

Such sweet purity, Jacqueline thinks as she pours water from a plastic measuring cup over Sylvie's thick black hair. Jacqueline massages shampoo that smells like lilacs into Sylvie's scalp. Sylvie stops moving and closes her eyes. She loves this part. Jacqueline examines her sun-browned face, her marred lips, the uneven tilt of her eyes. And all at once, Jacqueline feels the weight of mother love, dangerous, crashing, crushing; it takes her breath away. She comprehends in this simple act of hair washing what she's always known—that Sylvie will never be capable of looking after herself, never be able to navigate the world without her or the very least her sister, Lesa, at her side.

Sylvie opens her eyes as if on cue and Jacqueline looks into them searching for something that will ease the moment. Some silvery lining, however tarnished, some slim sliver of hope that says otherwise. How can Jacqueline keep her safe for an entire lifetime when she narrowly managed to save her from *that man* this afternoon?

Simply because she left coffee simmering on the stove? What kind of shaky providence is that? Certainly not the divine intervention of the God that Mary-Lynn mentioned earlier. How anyone can find solace in a God capable of such treachery and flimsy intercession eludes Jacqueline. Perhaps it's fear, out-and-out fear that keeps people in faith, keeps faith in check. The unknown worse than the known, however horrific that may be. She looks deep inside Sylvie's eyes to where the daughter of her dreams lies: lucid Sylvie, smart Sylvie, *safe* Sylvie, but Sylvie's darkness is as indecipherable as any God's.

Jacqueline pulls the plug and waits for Sylvie, who rolls stomach-down in their sea-green tub, following the mini cyclone of water as it twirls down the drain. Headed for the ocean, every last drop of it, Jacqueline tells her. When the cyclone is gone, Sylvie allows her mother to lift her, towel her off, pull on cotton underwear, cotton T-shirt, and carry her down the hall to her room. Jacqueline lays Sylvie on her metal-framed bed without turning on the light so as not to disrupt her sleepiness. Jacqueline sits in the dark, patting Sylvie's back, a nightly ritual. She sees a flash of lightning outside Sylvie's window, hears the sharp rupture of thunder not a second later. Goosebumps undulate along the surface of her freckled skin.

Wednesday, February 1973 » Lloyd, age 40

On the heels of younger, faster Constable Pete, Corporal Lloyd rounds the corner behind Neville's hotel. They wait while the inspector gets into his car, drives slowly, the odd townsperson on the street, otherwise not much else moving in this kind of weather. The snow has stopped, the sky low, socked-in, Frigidaire white. The north wind picking up so that Lloyd feels it penetrate his undershirt like pinpricks, tiny arrows of ice on his vulnerable skin. He left his parka in Neville's lounge. Damn stupid. He can't go back in case the inspector's not alone, nor can he risk the inspector finding him on the street—a simple Breathalyzer will do him in. The cold makes his thoughts thick, slow. Likely the inspector's in town for the night; he'll be staking out the detachment, waiting for Lloyd or Constable Pete to show up.

He looks at his watch, 1:15. It's only a matter of time before the vet's feline op wanders in for their 2:00 AM appointment and likewise the veterinarian wanders next door to the detachment looking for him. He's got to get Jimmy out of there. He won't send Constable Pete; he doesn't want Pete mixed up in his mess.

"Got your car today?" Lloyd asks Pete, who is standing with his back up against Neville's building out of the blasting cold wind.

"The wife has it. She's going to Warspite this afternoon for something or other." Constable Pete checks his watch. "She should still be home, want me to call?"

"That would be dandy, Pete."

Constable Pete goes the long way round to Neville's café while Lloyd watches the inspector drive across the street to the courthouse. He gets out and peers into the frosted windows of Lloyd's cruiser. The frost bodes well, Corporal Lloyd knows. Gives him the excuse of elongated business inside. The inspector goes into the courthouse. Lloyd can see him at the front desk, Doris Michelchuk's chocolate soufflé hair tilting this way and that. He's glad he called her a prize earlier, can only hope she misplaces her razor-sharp Rota memory on his whereabouts.

The inspector comes out. He glances back at Doris, who's standing at the courthouse window with her hands on her generous hips pointing down Main Street, her head nodding in the direction of the hardware store. Irritation etched on the inspector's face, he gets into his car and drives the opposite direction.

Corporal Lloyd smiles. He owes Doris one.

Constable Pete comes back, confirms that the car, his wife are accounted for. He's got Lloyd's parka and one leather glove.

"Who's on late shift?" Lloyd pulls the still-warm parka on, zips it up beneath his chin. No longer the cardamom smell of babies but the dank, fusty compulsion of Neville's lounge. He puts on the one glove, stuffs his other hand in his pocket.

"Boykos and Sasyniuk," says Constable Pete.

"Good, they can manage on their own."

Lloyd hands him the keys to the cruiser.

"Run me over to your car, then go out and visit the Fleck brothers. Tell them I need them at the detachment tomorrow morning, 9:00 AM sharp."

He knows the Fleck brothers won't show up. He hasn't got any real hard evidence against them beyond Jimmy Widman's word—there's not a shadow of doubt in Lloyd's mind where Jimmy is concerned, but he's seasoned enough to know Fleck democracy will rule in this case. He simply wants the Fleck boys to enjoy a sleepless night on his behalf.

"Will do," says Pete. "After that?"

"Stay home with your wife, it's too cold to go to Warspite today." He winks at Constable Pete, who flushes red.

Constable Pete jogs easily across the street to the courthouse, climbs into the cruiser, and starts it. Doris Michelchuk watches from the window. Constable Pete drives down the alley behind Neville's hotel. She waves at the two of them as they pull onto Main Street, then turn right down a back alley.

Wednesday, October 1987 » Lesa, age 31

When she's sure the coyote is dead, Lesa goes over, lays the Grim Reaper's cape across the animal's stock-still warm body, her own body cold, in shock. She shivers in the October trench, then lies down beside the coyote, as close as she dares to the infested animal. She can see fleas jumping ship as the host's body cools. She doesn't care. She runs her fingers along the bridge of the coyote's snout, the soft fur like velveteen, like the smooth skin on the inside of her mother's freckled arms. She feels the animal's heat extinguish completely, can no longer see its vaporous soul, imagined or otherwise. After a while she sits up, wipes her face with her numb hands, dusts the grey highway grit off her black Spandex, then claws her way back up the embankment to her mother's waiting car.

Mercifully the cigarette butt in the back seat has extinguished, but not before burning a perfectly symmetrical circle in the velour of her mother's car. Lesa glances once more at the lifeless coyote in the highway ditch. An image she'll conjure up days, nights, years from now, along with the image of her mother in her father's car, for the futile purpose of self-torment. Nothing she can change, but like certain troubling luggage it's perpetually transportable.

Lesa digs through her red suitcase, finds her blue jeans, white tennis shoes, her Moroccan sweater. She unzips her pleather boots, slides the jeans over her Spandex, pulls on the thick sweater, glad for the double layers, the warmth. Then she takes her boots, props them up against a mileage sign on the side of Highway 2, and plants the stiletto heels into the soft gravel in the off chance that the waitress from Carstairs might drive by and claim them. Someone needs to have a good/God Wednesday. She starts her mother's car and drives the rest of the way to Red Deer in the dead quiet.

Wednesday, July 1961 » Jacqueline, age 27

After patting Sylvie's back for a full three-quarters of an hour until her dark eyes finally gave in, cried uncle, closed, Jacqueline clicks the door shut ever so quietly and goes to retrieve Nate from the living room chesterfield. She carries Nate down the hall and lays him in the twin bed across from Lesa. She pulls the Fantastic Four sheet over Nate, glances across at Lesa, who, asleep, on top of her covers, is still fully dressed in her skort and blouse from this morning. Why didn't Lesa put her pyjamas on? Likely she didn't brush her teeth either after her makeshift dinner. Jacqueline examines the sprinkle of umber freckles across Lesa's nose like her own, a resolve to her jaw even in sleep. Jacqueline feels bad about the Wonder Bread and peanut butter. She didn't even have time to give Lesa a proper supper. What with young Nate and the mess on the living room carpet and the matter of Sylvie. A relentless constant in her life that she can't put out of her mind for a brief moment; even in her dreams Sylvie haunts her. Jacqueline knows Lesa gets the short straw. But she's tired, so full, it seems, of metal burrs these days.

Jacqueline sits down on the bed and soothes her palm over Lesa's lightly sunburnt cheeks, her smooth forehead. She shouldn't expect so much from her. She's five years old, a child. Though Lesa seems to have something that Sylvie responds to, a calming effect, a silent bond, an unconscious way of communicating like twins, perhaps it's their closeness in age. Jacqueline knows how heavily she relies on Lesa. It's not fair, but she doesn't know what else to do. She can't rely on her husband, and her mother, two provinces away, is of little use. She thought about calling her mother this afternoon, but the last conversation she had with her mother, her mother said, "You make your bed at dawn and every dusk you lie in." A twist Jacqueline hadn't heard before and wasn't quite sure what her mother meant by it either. Nothing good, she's sure. No, she doesn't need that right now. Her mother-in-law is even less useful; the sun rises but never sets on her only son.

Lesa stirs and rolls over. Jacqueline puts her hand on Lesa's back, considers gently waking her and then the two of them can go into the kitchen and share a midnight snack. She feels the day slipping from her tense shoulders. They are two women in this together, she thinks, not just now but for life. Such is the nature of women, be it fate or blight of genetics, she doesn't know which. They are the caregivers, the nurturers. She pushes Lesa's strawberry-blond bangs off her forehead. Exhales into the dark, would like to simply lie down beside Lesa and go to sleep too. But she knows she needs to eat something both for herself and the growing fetus in her uterus. She can't think of it as a baby, not yet, not with the possibility that it could be another Sylvie.

She tucks Nate's peach towel lightly over Lesa for when the rain comes and cools everything down. She forgives her utterly, completely.

On Lloyd's covert operation to the veterinarian's next to his RCMP detachment, he manages to move Jimmy Widman sight unseen into Constable Pete's post-pubescent, orange fluorescent '73 Camaro, a Z28 that has thick black racing stripes up the hood and down the back of the car. Hardly the unobtrusive getaway car Lloyd wanted, but a car nonetheless. Likely the inspector is still wandering the town in search of him, but Lloyd's not immediately worried. He's got friends in many places. He fishes through his breast pocket and finds a leftover El Producto from earlier this morning, so long ago it seems like days have passed, but still it's Wednesday. He pushes the lighter in, waits for the quiet metal click in between Jimmy's sporadic mouth breathing from the back seat that sounds like a spouting whale, a regular Moby Dick. He lights his cigar.

As he skirts along the unpaved lane in front of his detachment, he checks to see if Jacqueline's at the kitchen window, smoking, doing the dishes, gazing blankly at the prairie outside. An endless flat earth void covered in white then wheat then white then wheat, year in year out, relentless in its unvarying cycle. What Jacqueline searches for, Lloyd doesn't know. Not him, he knows, she gave up the search years ago. The children, yes. Always the children for Jacqueline. When they were younger, they ventured bravely across this expansive field to the windbreak where the black and white magpies built their sizeable bowl-shaped nests in the crooks of the poplar trees. The magpie nests, a messy mass of sticks and stones and leaves and twigs and thorny branches tangled up in the stripped-down arms of the winter trees. The nests large and dark and complicated. So ominous in the distance that Nate and Clare and Lesa imagined them dead bodies bundled in the trees—but, no, only the barbed mess of their chaotic quarters.

He glances once more at the kitchen window refracting the white field, the white sky, the white cloud ever-present in Lloyd's sleep-deprived mind, some distant past. The cloud surrounding his Sylvie, his Jacqueline—his unspeakable absence. His past versus Jacqueline's presence versus their future, a single cold blue imprint stamped on Lloyd's horizon. He wishes Jacqueline were at the window so he could see her. But she's not. Insular now, interior, as if when Sylvie left a part of Jacqueline went with her, not unlike the live wire pulsing at low frequency beneath Lloyd's pale skin— insular, unremitting, a constant reminder whether he likes it or not.

He turns out onto the secondary highway that takes him south.

» » »

Lloyd cranes his stiff neck, twenty hours into his shift, can hardly stay awake at the wheel. Will have to stop along the way to find coffee and food for both himself and Jimmy. No cars in sight, nothing to see here but the frozen white prairies that span the distance to an equally pallid horizon. A bleak glacial landscape with the northern wind cleaving across it. Lloyd pulls the napkin from his shirt pocket and glances over it. Funny that Judge Wade chose Michener over Ponoka, which is the closer of the two government-run mental institutions. Perhaps Ponoka is not admitting at the moment. He hopes the handwritten napkin is good enough, weighty enough for the present until they can properly admit Jimmy Widman.

Lloyd checks his rear-view mirror: Jimmy cleaned up, stitched up, neatly jawed, is curled in the back seat of Pete's Camaro in a woman's powder blue ski suit. He looks as if he's ready to head out skiing as they drive south toward Red Deer, and farther on the Rockies in the distance that stretch down to the Montana border and beyond. The *beautiful fucking* Rockies, Lloyd recalls Lesa pointing out when she was only eight years of age as they drove to Montana one year. Lloyd smiles at the thought, takes a puff of his rank cigar. Without taking the dense smoke into his lungs, he exhales out the slightly rolled-down window.

"You with me, Jimmy?"

Jimmy spouts Moby-like, whimpers canine as he rolls on the back seat. His broken ribs bound tight by the doctor. Smells like dog shampoo, and something else too, Lloyd thinks. The heady scent of jasmine, perhaps? Lloyd inhales deeply, yes, Chanel No. 5. He's sure of it, the kind Jacqueline used to wear. Lloyd pictures Jacqueline: young, vital, essential, her coppery red hair piled on top of her head, her violet eyes glossy with promise. And him too, young, strong, thick black brush cut, the glimmer train of his potential in his dark flashing eyes like the polished metal buttons down the front of his red serge. Between the two of them their entire world a shimmer, a sparkle, a shine like it was only yesterday. The scent of Jacqueline present in his car, his nostrils, the warm memory of her close in his mind. He should be able to reach out and touch it, as concrete and tangible as he and Jacqueline once were, no longer seem to be.

He stubs his cigar out in the ashtray, remembers his children, small, hugging his neck tightly, Nate whispering goodbyes that tickled his ear and made him laugh. And from Sylvie even, the rare odd hug that stuck with him for months afterward. Lesa and Clare clinging to his navy pants with the familiar yellow RCMP stripe, unable to let him go. The entire lot of them: his world, his wife, his children, his life on a glorious half-shell, waving and blowing kisses on the front step of the row housing where they used to live, like he was leaving for good but simply for work. Over the years the long hours, the gradual drift: exhausted wives, preoccupied husbands, children in worlds of their own who barely noticed whether he was there or gone. It feels like forever ago, like someone else's dream entirely.

Lloyd shudders with the cold leaking in from the partially opened window. He rolls it up, glances into the back seat at Jimmy Widman, curled, sleeping again. His mashed face, his mouth agape, eye stitched and swollen, a nasty bruise forming beneath his jaw. He hopes to God Jimmy Widman's sleeping dreams are better than his waking ones.

Wednesday, October 1987 » Lesa, age 31

Her black Spandex beneath her jeans, changed into tennis shoes
and Moroccan sweater, Lesa's storm is half over. Her mind no
longer addled from the partial joint, the early morning flight, too
much coffee, not enough sleep, the impossibility of Mr. Green, her
mother, the dead coyote. She finds herself in Red Deer, not entirely
cognizant of having driven the long, lulling stretch from Carstairs
on. She crawls along on Gaetz Avenue, the 10:30 AM traffic slowed
by construction or perhaps an accident up ahead. So that when she
should have turned right onto 32nd Avenue, she didn't. Instead she
followed the slow-moving line of mostly pickup trucks through the
centre of town, ending up on the bridge. She didn't remember a
bridge or the river the last time they came to see Sylvie. Could be
she missed her turn?

The traffic stopped, only one lane open, the other three closed
for bridge construction. She realizes her error. She watches the Red
Deer River below while she waits. The water fast, flowing, deep, brilliant blue despite the weak October light. Brings to mind something
about rivers from a philosophy course she took at UBC. Everything
flows, nothing stands still? Same river/different man? Too much

water, not enough man? Never good at sayings or philosophy, Lesa studies the river, thinks instead of her father. Too much water under the bridge? No, it's not that either. Nor does she believe that where her father is concerned.

When she learned of her father's illness, shortly before she graduated from high school, then she spent his remaining years learning him. Who he was, why he was, where he'd come from, where he was going, where he ended up. Not a perfect human being by any standards. Certainly not the kind of husband she will choose, but surely, despite his dalliances, surely he must have loved Lesa's mother? Hard to believe, but why else would they stay together? On the outside their marriage as temporary as basted seams, but on the inside, who knows what private sutures stitched them one to the other? The children perhaps, Sylvie, shared grief? Lesa can't surmise. All she knows is that as a father he couldn't have loved them all more.

She waits on the stalled bridge, wishes her father were still here, still the suspension between Lesa and her mother. When he died three years ago, their bridge collapsed entirely, leaving Lesa heartsick, rootless, and drifting from one boyfriend to the next in Vancouver, frantic in her loneliness, desperate to fill the recesses that even now feel bottomless. And on the prairies, her mother, alone, silently desperate—the two women remote, divided by the fucking Rockies, isolated in their grief over her father.

The line of traffic moves slowly over the bridge. Lesa glances to her right and spots the white façade of the Michener administration building on the hill this side of the river. Damn, she's missed her second chance to turn. Now she'll have to circle back around. The traffic slouches along. Eventually she clears the construction, loops back around, then waits once more in the lineup heading across the same bridge, different river to retrace her steps to Michener. She keeps her sight on the white facade lest she forget what she came for. Never forget, never forgotten. There it is, she thinks, everything and nothing.

Lesa watches the dark blue water rush below, longs for accelerated bridges, live fathers, mended mothers.

Wednesday, July 1961 » Jacqueline, age 27

Jacqueline wanders down the hall to check on Sylvie once more before she lies down on the sofa. She will not sleep with her husband tonight. Perhaps never again. She hasn't made that decision yet. All she wants to do is get through to the morning and see how things look then. She peers into Sylvie's tiny, holding-cell-sparse room, illuminated by the yellow glow of her night light. Sylvie isn't in her bed. Her covers are pushed down to the bottom of her bed, nothing special about that as Sylvie often thrashes about while dead asleep. But where is Sylvie? Once she's down for the night, she's rarely wakes until 4:00 or 5:00 AM. Seldom does she wander from her room. She can't hide in the closet because Jacqueline keeps it locked so Sylvie doesn't take all her clothes out and then pile them on the floor and urinate on them like a coyote marking territory. No dresser to crouch behind due to Sylvie's penchant for climbing anything. Jacqueline was afraid that with Sylvie's remarkable strength, she might push the dresser across the room to the window. She had Lloyd move it out into the hallway. No, nothing in Sylvie's room but the single metal-framed bed that she hasn't managed to pull apart thus far—the bed, but no body.

Jacqueline feels the bile rise from her empty stomach. It didn't occur to her until now, until this exact moment. *What if? What if* the man came back? The scar on the man's right cheek, his hard eyes and inverted teeth flash across her mind as clear as the burst of sheet lightning that illuminates the room then. As clear as if *that man* is standing in some murky corner of Sylvie's room, or under the bed with Sylvie beside him, his large hand covering her crooked mouth. Or possibly the front door is wide open and they are already gone. Jacqueline flips the light on. Nothing. She runs down the hall to the living room, her head woozy from exhaustion, nausea, lack of food. She trips on their lime-green ottoman. She reaches out to catch herself on the hi-fi cabinet and accidentally turns it on as her body hits the floor. Ted Daffan and the Texans' scratchy 1944 hit. His dark, mournful voice, liquid in her ears as she lies on the damp carpet. He sings into the black of her living room.

Where does her husband find these outdated records? How many times has she lain in bed listening to her born-too-loose, intoxicated husband, crooning along to that song? Like an alcoholic's national anthem. Where her husband finds solace, she can't imagine. Jacqueline's throat tightens. Not until now has she allowed herself the thought or even the idea that anyone could be born into this life to lose. But fresh with fear roiling in the pit of her belly, stirring in her uterus, she thinks of Sylvie and considers otherwise. She sees tiny lights shimmer like fragmented stars before her eyes; her head light, dizzy. She might pass out. She's weary, so goddamn, born-to-lose weary. She could lie here in their identical row housing on their worn-out carpet amid the damp vomit and her children's Lego, with no one, not even her husband, to save her from the wreckage.

She hears Lesa yelp from her bedroom.

"It's all right, Lesa," she croaks, "It's just the hi-fi."

Lesa doesn't reply. She might be sleep talking.

Jacqueline regains her head, pulls her heavy body up slowly, turns off the Texans.

She listens in the silence for Sylvie's insistent chatter, but hears nothing. Then she sees the light from the kitchen. Hadn't she turned that off when she put Nate to bed?

Every hair on her body is raised. She hobbles across the room, avoiding the overturned footstool. When she reaches the light, the doorway, she listens again. Now she hears Sylvie's soft breathing like a sigh, her chatter more subdued than normal. She hesitates. What if Sylvie is not alone in the kitchen? Swiftness and surprise are the key, this she knows from her husband's work. It's the only chance she has. She breathes shallowly, readying herself to burst into the room like a lone-woman Emergency Response Team.

Sylvie spins past the doorway in the kitchen.

What is she doing?

Jacqueline peers sideways into the room. The deadbolt on the back door is secure, windows closed; no one is in the kitchen but Sylvie, twirling about like a ballerina in the yellow light with a butter knife and the jar of peanut butter that Lesa forgot to put back in their childproof cupboards. Jacqueline's relief is audible, but as swift as it comes, it dissolves. Like the relief she feels when her husband comes home after his shift. He's alive! she thinks each time, but then the moment is flattened by the smell of Crown Royal on his breath, the awful scent of another woman inexplicably on his body.

Sylvie is eating the peanut butter straight from the jar. Worse, peanut butter is everywhere: on the countertop, the table, smeared on the cupboards, across the black-and-white checkers of their linoleum, painted over the walls like Sylvie does with her feces in the bathroom if Jacqueline doesn't catch her in time. Jacqueline could kill Lesa for leaving the peanut butter out. That is, as soon as she gets Sylvie under control.

Sylvie doesn't stop when she sees her mother but continues to alternately lick the butter knife and then swirl the peanut butter on the countertop with her slender fingers. Her black hair is wild, askew in brown clumps. She has peanut butter on her hands, up her arms, down her legs, and if this weren't the camel's last straw or Jacqueline's also—if under different circumstances, a day other than today—Jacqueline might run and grab the Brownie and capture this snapshot of Sylvie for later, for laughter, for memory, for the posterity of her children, for her delinquent husband to see.

"Sylvie!" she yells before she remembers not to.

Sylvie's dark eyes go wide, feral. She drops the butter knife on the floor and bolts around her mother into the living room. Jacqueline knows that in a matter of seconds Sylvie will have covered the entire living room in peanut butter.

All Jacqueline feels is monster, intentional.

There is no point in chasing Sylvie. Futile. Sylvie is quick, agile, and can easily evade her. Instead Jacqueline goes down the hall to her bedroom, sits on the unmade bed, lights a Peter Jackson, inhales as severely as her lungs will allow. She can hear Sylvie moving about in the living room, no doubt rubbing the peanut butter from her hands onto the back of the chesterfield. With each cavernous intake of nicotine, she feels her fury subside. Instead the *dis*-ease takes over, reeling through her veins the strange deadening of morphine—the gentle narcotic slip of an undertow. This Wednesday has been building since seven this morning, Jacqueline thinks, since Sylvie was first born.

It's as if someone else is in charge now, someone she doesn't recognize. Someone whose children are all normal, manageable, reasonable, with a husband who comes home every night without the second-hand smell of liquor and secondary women on his body that she longs to cling to despite everything.

Her cigarette ash drops to the floor. She doesn't care. Light the house on fire and she wouldn't care either. She thinks about *that man* still out there lying in wait. If not for her Sylvie, then some other vulnerable child. She thinks about her husband, also out there, in the arms, the bed of some other woman. Another other. And despite the fetus and the fear living as one in her belly, she realizes that while she no longer *wants* her husband—whether by God, or by the sheer luminosity of their children, she *needs* him. The two are twisted up like electrical wires, complicated and live.

The shame that she cannot do without him is crushing, makes her want, no, *need* to get down on her knees in the dark and pray. She slips off the bed onto the floor. But to whom, whom can she pray? How do you pray to a God capable of such duplicity? How could anyone? She cannot do this alone. She needs someone to believe in, someone to blame. She doesn't drive, hasn't worked in eight years. What kind of job would she get anyway? A telephone operator on night shift like she did before she got married? How could she care for the children then? Besides that, where would she and the children live? Who would look after the new baby? She doesn't know. She's down to the burnt filter of her cigarette, down also to elemental despair, suddenly stripped down and terrified. She doesn't know anything anymore.

She stabs her cigarette out in the ashtray next to the bed. She listens in the black for Sylvie. She can't hear her. Sylvie must have exhausted herself, peanut butter being the sleep elixir. White light flashes across the bedroom window followed closely by the crack of thunder. Too close, she thinks. It reminds her that the outside world is hazardous, beyond her, beyond the primal fetus in her uterus. Certainly beyond Sylvie. Possibly beyond God?

She gets up, feels the metal burrs collect beneath her mother-skin: assemble, align, form barbed wire. Jacqueline knows what she needs to do.

North of Edmonton, Lloyd pulls into the Burger Baron, rolls down his window. The frigid air invades the warmth of Pete's Camaro, causing every hair on Lloyd's body to rise at once despite the bulk of his RCMP parka, the layers of clothing beneath, the beige shirt his wife presses for him each Sunday, the undershirts she bleaches. The unwelcome cold forms bumps along the surface of his skin.

"Can I help you?" says an impatient female voice through the metal speaker, which shakes Lloyd from his reverie, the inward cold.

Lloyd peruses the menu but can't make out the beef from the chicken from the fries from the onion rings due to the white frost assaulting the faded coloured images: the pictures like memory itself waning with age, light, time.

"*Sir?* We close at seven," the disembodied voice says.

Lloyd looks at his watch, just past two. Smart-ass.

"In that case," Lloyd says, "give me a black coffee, whatever the Burger Baron special is, and fries, times two."

"Hot chocolate?" he asks Jimmy.

Jimmy Widman is sitting outright upright now. A good sign. Jimmy grunts. Lloyd takes that for a yes.

"Whipped cream with that, *sir*?"

Her sirs like cider vinegar.

Lloyd ignores the tone, turns and looks at Jimmy, his dishevelled hair, the powder blue ski suit, the warp of his distorted face that Lloyd never really noticed before. Easy to overlook whenever he found Jimmy slumped over, lying face down, taking refuge in some abandoned doorway like a child's fort. Lloyd thought it had to do with too many impromptu ditch fights with the Fleck brothers but recognizes instinctively Sylvie's skewed features, the backward slant of eyes, the twisted hairline scar intersecting Jimmy's lips, notwithstanding his broken nose, dislocated jaw, stitches, swelling, bruising, battering et al., the unnatural intensity in his one eye as if to make up for everything else Jimmy has had to withstand in his forty difficult years.

"God, yes, give the man whipped cream, please," Lloyd says.

Lloyd hears the abrupt click of the speaker. He laughs. In the back seat Jimmy Widman rubs his smooth hands together. Nice to see him alive, awake, receptive.

Lloyd pulls the Camaro forward. The disembodied woman from the speaker stands by the closed window tallying Lloyd's order on the side of a foldout box. Lloyd studies the paper napkin from Judge Wade, which he hopes will suffice. He hasn't got many options left. He waits for the woman to open the window, studies her face. The woman's face like her voice, acidic, wearied, carved out like an aging farmer, too many bad years, failed crops, older and nothing much to show for it. He knows the look, has seen it in Jacqueline's eyes, his own.

"Six dollars, fifty-eight cents, sir," the woman says, her breath visible white in the frigid air.

Lloyd passes her a twenty. Her thin eyes run over the RCMP insignia on his parka, the thick black racing stripes up the hood of Pete's orange Camaro. Jimmy, battered and suspect in the back seat. She raises her brow but doesn't ask. Nor does Lloyd offer. Nonetheless it doesn't change a thing between them, just another order, another customer, the woman overaged and underemployed at Burger Baron. And Lloyd, status-clad as he is in his navy RCMP parka, is tired, bone weary as this Wednesday is long.

Jimmy pushes the passenger seat forward, tries to manoeuvre the door handle.

"Where you headed, Jimmy?"

"Bathroom," Jimmy slurs.

Lloyd leans over, helps Jimmy open the passenger door.

"Make sure you come right back," Lloyd says, surveying the vast nothingness of the frozen prairie around them, the stand-alone Burger Baron. No place really to go.

Jimmy gets out, winks his one good eye at Corporal Lloyd.

Amazing he can even walk, considering, Lloyd thinks, and shuts the door to keep the heat in.

Lloyd hangs his hand out the window to retrieve his change from the woman.

"Waiting on the fries," she says, handing over his change, then snaps the take-out window shut before Lloyd can thank her.

Lloyd rolls his window up, glances over the restaurant to locate Jimmy, but he's nowhere in sight. Must be in the men's room. A few older men sit in the plain wood booths sipping coffee from Styrofoam cups reading the *Edmonton Journal* likely, not much else news-wise going on north of the province's capital. Over in the corner, a birthday party in progress, for a girl from the looks of the bright pink and red shiny balloons. The gaggle of smiling, laughing children, their warm-faced mothers. Helium balloons in abundance, tied to the tables in bunches, around the kids' skinny wrists, floating in a row along the top of the coat rack, a veritable balloon fest.

Oddly, sadly, it makes him think of Sylvie. All he ever wanted for her. All any father wants for their children: bright, shiny, floating on top of this world happy. Or at the very least, a solid chance at it. Not too much to ask for, is it? He envisions Sylvie housed in Michener, imprisoned in her own mind. Hopes to some charitable God that's not the case. Hopes instead she possesses the fleeting memory of a goldfish. Doesn't recollect her family on each loop around her large shared bedroom. Around the fish bowl of the small crowded day room at Michener. Lloyd hopes she has no recollection whatsoever: of Jacqueline, their two-door Plymouth Fury, his unpardonable absence. The swift chill beneath Lloyd's shirt has nothing to do with the weather.

He wills himself to quit thinking, watches the birthday children chase one another around the Burger Baron in between french fry breaks, gulps of pop, hugs from their mothers, a simple game of child's tag.

Lloyd glances at his watch, almost 2:30. They'd better get a move on if he's going to get to Michener before the administration office closes at 4:30. Wouldn't do him or Jimmy Widman any good to have to spend the night in Red Deer. Besides that, there's anxiousness in the pit of his belly, something to do with the day, getting home to Jacqueline, his children, some part of him not ready to face Sylvie after all this time.

He rolls down his window, knocks on the drive-thru to get the older woman's attention. He can't see her. But over by the coat rack with the plethora of birthday balloons taped above it, he spots Jimmy in his powder blue ski suit with his back to him. He's jerking about. What is he doing? Lloyd hopes it's not some sort of standing seizure. Though he knows from Sylvie that's not possible. Petit mal, yes, but anything grand would require the full co-operation of the body and always on the floor. Maybe an after-effect to hypothermia that Lloyd doesn't know about? Jesus Christ, will this day never end?

Lloyd raps sharply on the takeout window, rouses the attention of one of the birthday mothers, young, pretty, dark short hair, pleasing green eyes. She smiles at Lloyd, waves. Lloyd doesn't know if she's waving at him, his RCMP-ness, or the Z28 Camaro, all things being equal, or so he imagines.

From his vantage point in the Camaro he can see Jimmy from the waist up, and whatever Jimmy's busy with over there in the corner by the coat rack, it must be enthralling because he can't get Jimmy to notice him.

"Goddamn." He shuts the motor off, climbs out of the car; the affront of the burning cold seizes his breath. He zips up his parka. And all at once, at precisely the same time, Lloyd sees, too, what the pretty mother, the other mothers, their gaggle of children, the men reading newspaper, the acidic woman who has reappeared— he sees what they see. They all watch Jimmy's back: the ski pants dropped around his ankles. His legs, two pale-coloured sticks like flamingos. The flat of his exposed buttocks, the accompanying herky-jerky motion.

Lloyd sees the young mother's face in a muted howl through

the closed window of the Burger Baron as he bolts to the entrance. Hopes he can get there in time, avert an all-out disaster. The children scrambling back to their mothers, the older men rising from the wood booths, but not one makes a move toward Jimmy. He could be live, like a grenade, go off unexpectedly. And Jimmy, Jimmy Widman in all his glory, in his women's ski suit, the shiny pink and red birthday balloons, full, round, curved in such a way that the colour pales ever so slightly at the peak of each balloon like delicate nipples. Not one, not a pair, but ten, fifteen, twenty almost bursting, rousing balloons floating in the over-heated air above the coat rack.

At the last possible moment, and before Lloyd is able to traverse the short distance across the restaurant, Jimmy Widman turns his head, no doubt in response to the combined wailing of children and mothers alike. Jimmy turns for the grand finale. His closing moment, the pin from his live grenade. He smiles eagerly, innocently at the birthday crowd, the men, the vinegar-faced woman with the hot chocolate in her hand, his whipped cream a mile high. He ejaculates onto the concrete floor of the Burger Baron.

Like breasts, is all Lloyd can think of as he tackles Jimmy to the floor, broken ribs and jaw, hypothermia aside. *Good Christ Almighty, who thought that up?*

Wednesday, October 1987 » Lesa, age 31

Lesa parks her mother's Toyota in the handicap spot in front of the administration building at Michener. She's not sure where exactly to find Sylvie. She may have to run inside and find out. She surveys the immaculate grounds gone winter yellow. Such an extravagant sprawl of space you rarely see in cities these days. Oddly reserved for the invisible, forgotten people inside Michener, her sister Sylvie included.

She recalls in past times these grounds were filled with men, women, children, fourteen hundred strong across the meticulously kept grounds. Deceptively open, no fences or barriers separating Michener from the magnificent sway of willow, fir, and birch trees in between. The winding paths and picnic tables, sun chairs and children's playground, the suburban neighbourhoods adjacent. Stark contrast to the locked-down brick buildings, the metal-barred windows. All the aberrant bright-faced children housed within. She's since learned the ABCs of mental illness: autistic, bipolar, compulsive, Down syndrome. The order and disorder of the impulsive, the obsessive, the paranoid and schizoid—and the catch-all when none of the other labels would suffice: the clinically depressed, too many of them children.

She climbs reluctantly out of her mother's car, not ready to go inside yet. Her distant memory of Michener some same sad river. Lesa sinks down on the curb, feels a sharp stab in her right lung, hopes she hasn't fractured something from her ditch roll. She tests each rib gingerly with her fingertips, though the ache seems to be deeper, interior. She worries about her marijuana use, her half-a-pack-a-day cigarette habit. Possibly that? She wonders if she's imagining it? She doesn't know—could be the whole place makes her achy inside, clinically depressed.

She pulls out a John, lights it in spite of herself.

Mostly it's the children, the beleaguered children Lesa can't forget. Their medicated, glassy eyes skipping over one another crowded thirty-odd in an eight-by-ten room, one worn-out caregiver in their numbers. The confused, perplexed faces of the children. Why were they here? Where were their parents? Their families, their brothers and sisters? Who were all these strangers? Or perhaps those were the questions that eddied through Lesa's childhood mind the few times they made the pilgrimage to see Sylvie after she was admitted.

The details of those few pilgrimages: her father silent, morose, waiting outside in their Plymouth Fury with young Nate and baby Clare. While Lesa, neither young enough to remain behind nor old enough to comprehend, went inside with her mother. Her mother's large dark sunglasses that hid the tears that trickled off her high cheekbones, spilled down her face regardless when she spotted Sylvie sitting at a table filling sheets of lined paper with meticulous rows upon rows of circles within circles within circles. The antithesis of Sylvie herself. And for Lesa that same past image of Sylvie embedded in her cells like DNA: Sylvie delicate-shouldered, dark-eyed, oddly quiet in the middle of the room. While all around her, the room was teeming with people, rocking in every corner, every chair, gesturing wildly behind the secured windows. People on the move, their hands and arms flailing in perpetual motion, moving silent, loud mouths. The combined gabble of the young/old/male/female.

Her sister Sylvie frozen in time, perfectly still in this space—oblivious to the chaotic, catatonic nightmare around her. The alien closed culture of the mentally ill hidden from public view in a government institution. Or so it seemed to young Lesa.

And later in the car, her father would take them to Dairy Queen, and they went inside and ordered a round of french fries and root beer, chocolate-dipped cones as if in celebration of Sylvie—of her new life away from theirs. Her father looked across the orange plastic booth at her mother, tried to smooth his hand over hers on the table. Only her mother pulled away, tucked her hand on Nate's soft belly, played the elusive surface of Clare's baby face. Only once did she leave it there that Lesa could recall. Years beyond those days at Michener, after her father had been diagnosed with the covert cancer that occupied him from the inside out in silent military precision. Then he reached across their kitchen table for her. Her mother's hand beneath her father's. The resigned look of some unvoiced sadness in both their eyes. And then, only then, could they forget, forgive themselves for a short time, go back to some semblance of married life for my father's remaindered time. Not uncomplicated, never easy, but necessary in some way.

Lesa takes a final drag from her cigarette, feels the insular pain deep in her lung, knows she's not imaging it. She may have to give up smoking altogether. She flicks her cigarette butt into the flowerbed in the front of building, among the tall dried stalks of poppies, the colourless dead chrysanthemums. Remembers the bright bit of Sylvie's face—that almost serene gap between everything that was going on around her, her parents, and Michener. She remembers the river, she remembers the adage: You cannot step into the same river twice.

She's not sure that's true. Yesterday's river is still raging, deep and silent, bleak despite the brilliant surface.

The concrete cold beneath her, Lesa stands up outside the administration building, willing but unable to will herself inside. She sees the curl of smoke from her discarded cigarette thickening. The smoke changing from white to yellow as the desiccated flowers catch on. She watches through eyes half shut, and just at that moment when the smouldering is no longer a magician's smokescreen, but the real thing, fire and heat, the heart of the matter, Lesa sprints across the lawn, stamps out the hungry flames beneath her white tennis shoes.

Perhaps the same sad river but not the same woman.

Wednesday, July 1961 » Jacqueline, age 27

Coldly, methodically, the *dis*-ease in full control now, with intent, as if she had thought it out meticulously in her head, planned, deliberate, premeditated, but no, the idea hadn't occurred to her until this precise moment: a solution, reprieve, respite. She walks through the dead quiet of the house with purpose she hasn't felt in years. Lesa and Nate are sleeping in their room. Sylvie, peanut butter and all, has fallen asleep next to the tartan chesterfield on the living room carpet among the drying Lego. Jacqueline goes into her bedroom, pulls down two of her husband's beige RCMP shirts that she irons every Sunday night for the week ahead while the children watch *Walt Disney Presents* on the television. Then she goes into the kitchen and fishes around in the orange ceramic bowl by the sink for the keys to her husband's '57 Plymouth Fury. She doesn't drive. He mostly drives the company cruiser.

Jacqueline tiptoes down the hall so as not to wake Lesa or Nate, peers into the dim light of Sylvie's room. The lone bed, the locked closet, the windows she had her husband reinforce shut so Sylvie couldn't climb out at night. No pictures on the walls for Sylvie to pull down and possibly smash the glass when the black moods,

Jacqueline calls them, overtake her. Then there is nothing to be done but hold the bedroom door shut knowing Sylvie's safe inside and wait it out until she falls into a shattered heap on the floor. Then Jacqueline goes in and sits on the floor, holds Sylvie in her arms until she quietens, returns to the present world. The bleak austerity of Sylvie's room not so different from the holding cells at the RCMP barracks.

God, that's depressing.

God?

She's tired.

She needs someone to hold her in his arms.

Jacqueline pushes her dishevelled hair off her face, realizes she hasn't so much as brushed her hair today let alone her teeth. Her stomach reels with fresh nausea, perhaps the anticipation of a resolution made. For a brief moment she feels buoyant. Almost, but then the import of her decision pulls her back down. She treads softly into the living room where Sylvie is snoring lightly on the carpet. Jacqueline sifts through the magazines, comic books on the coffee table, finds her cigarettes, lights another in the dark. She smokes standing. She doesn't want to sit. She's doesn't want anything to impede this last momentum, this final bit of courage, despair that she feels in the pit of her stomach along with the unknown of her unborn child. She watches Sylvie, her breath calm, measured, deep in sleep. Jacqueline inhales, exhales in sync.

She takes a last drag, drops her cigarette into her leftover coffee from this morning. The cigarette hisses, sends up a poof of smoke like a magician's trick in order to distract the audience from the real action, the real trick she is about to perform.

In the bedroom closet she unhooks the flexible hose from the Electrolux vacuum, then pulls down one of her husband's neatly pressed shirts and walks back through the silent house into their attached single garage. She stuffs the pressed shirt into one tail pipe, then pushes the vacuum hose into the other tailpipe of his Plymouth Fury, a two-door sports coupe model. He didn't even have the sense to buy a four-door. She threads the hose through the back window, does the window up as much as she can. She slides in the driver side. The vinyl seats sticky with the impending thunderstorm. Jacqueline puts the keys in the ignition, hesitates for a moment, a crucial split second in which things could go either way, wholly irreparable, or else largely unnoticed like the thousands of splintered thoughts that pass through her head on any given day except for today, this Wednesday in mid-July.

With intent she starts the car, leans across and rolls the passenger window up tight, cranes her neck around to see that the windows in the back are also done up. She turns the heater on full, goes back into the house.

Wednesday, February 1973 » Lloyd, age 40

Corporal Lloyd has Jimmy Widman pinned to the concrete floor of
the Burger Baron, minimizing any further damage that Jimmy may
have to offend this small community. At least that's the hope. Lloyd
feels winter seeping through the cement in direct opposition to the
sated heat coming off Jimmy's body like a smouldering campfire.
The pandemonium in the restaurant is fever pitch: sobbing children,
crying mothers, the older men shaking their heads like they'd seen it
all before, but wait, not yet, here's something new to go home with
to tell their shocked wives. Balloons, go figure.

Lloyd figures the logistics in his fatigued head. A room full
of people, Jimmy half-naked beneath him and squirming to be
released—how to get him out? He looks up to see vinegar-faced
woman standing above them, her indignant hands perched on her
wide hips, glaring down as if she knew from the start he was trouble
in his '73 Camaro Z28 with the battered suspect passenger in the
back seat. As if she can't believe he brought this powder blue ski-suit-
packaged repulsion and the flimsy excuse of his RCMP parka upon
them, at a birthday party no less. Lloyd thanks Christ he's still in
uniform or things could be worse, much worse.

Nothing left to do but attend to the already seen crime scene and follow procedure. Lloyd hauls Jimmy to his feet, instructs the crowd to step back, though everyone is spread out in a circle as far away as the walls of the Burger Baron will allow. Young mothers clutching their young children, shielding their innocent eyes; no one wants anything to do with it, but given the sudden absurdity of the situation, they don't have much choice. Certainly not something Lloyd could anticipate, no prior behaviour that he knows where Jimmy is involved. He wonders if Judge Wade had anything like this before his bench. He'd have to ask him, also make mention of it to the Michener people. No balloons, please.

But no one is hurt here. Certainly Jimmy meant no malice, intended no harm, just an erratic child's impulse, and nothing to do with the children, everything to do with balloons, however X-rated it may appear to the stunned onlookers, obliged by his adult body. Hard to reconcile where the birthday children are concerned, but given some distance over time, coffee gossip being what it is, this could conceivably go down in history as one of those things you didn't see coming but got to anyway.

With Jimmy's hands secured in cuffs behind his back, not that Lloyd believes Jimmy is a danger in any way, the handcuffs more for the sake of the mothers, the wailing children, the indignant Burger Baron woman, Lloyd shields Jimmy's emaciated body while he pulls the ski pants up and fastens the silver heart clasp around his waist. Jimmy's warm skin flushed the colour of the pink balloons, the shut black eye, his excited, distended face, rough stitches across his left brow. His cauliflower ear, too long someone's punching bag. The balloons float languidly above Jimmy, above the coat rack as if

148

nothing happened, ready to continue on with the birthday party. The room calmer, under control now, less wailing, sobbing, streaked tears drying on the children's faces. The grateful mothers reassured by the All-Canadian Dudley Do-Right to the rescue (no idea that what Jimmy inflicted on them was indirectly Lloyd's doing). The dark-haired mother smiles at Corporal Lloyd, who hangs on tight to Jimmy as he steers him across the restaurant, stopping to pick up their order and Jimmy's hot chocolate from the counter, no chance whatsoever for a repeat performance.

Offside outside the Burger Baron, Lloyd slides the handcuffs off Jimmy, guides him gently into the back seat of the Z28. Jimmy rubs his wrists, his chin to his chest. Lloyd turns the ignition, the 383 Crate engine roars to life. The Burger Baron woman scowls out the window at the pair of them, the rough rumble of Constable Pete's Hedman headers confirming what the woman already knew.

Jimmy leans into the front seat.

"Jimmy's in the soup, huh?" he says, his face close to Corporal Lloyd's, the smack of Wild Turkey mixed with the faint trace of antiseptic, dog shampoo, semen.

Lloyd can't help but smile beneath his parka. Funny in a way that only Lloyd can locate in this moment. Knowing, also, it's the only thing that keeps him on the job—the searching, finding, in fact requiring the humour, the tinfoil lining, however crumpled or tarnished in any number of the unforeseen, bizarre circumstances that Lloyd comes up against. Because the times when neither humour nor tinfoil are present, it makes the job unbearable.

Wednesday, October 1987 » Lesa, age 31

Traversing the straight road that connects the south side of Michener to the north, Lesa sees the military precision of the flat-topped brick buildings laid out in a long row on Medley Drive. The first building, the windows are heavily barred, same with the doors. Reserved for the dangerously ill, the high behaviours, the clients within escorted by paired staff, usually men. She knows Sylvie was never housed there. She walks along the wide swath of sidewalk in front of the buildings, the October air brisk on her face, reaching beneath her Alpaca sweater to her already chilled skin. She hugs her body for warmth, hopes her childhood instincts will kick in, give her some intuitive familial signal that she's found the right building, the place where Sylvie resides. When she gets to the end of the row with no such insight, she goes around to the back, hoping that might trigger some past recollection.

The invisible sun even more so on the backside of the buildings, the faint shadows barely purple on the yellowed lawns, the air distinctively colder. She stands a moment surveying her surroundings: the brick buildings look identical, though she knows from early experience, from the identical row housing they used to live in, from her parents slanted marriage, she knows that looks can be deceiving.

Arbitrarily she chooses 218B, this door open to outsiders but closed to the residents inside. The lukewarm smell of hospital food assaults her nostrils, beneath that, the floor wax, bleach, the thin trace of human urine. The main floor corridor is empty, save for the second set of doors that Lesa knows will fully admit/commit her to Michener. If she enters those, then she is officially locked in and can't get out without a staff member to release her. She stands on the tips of her tennis shoes and peers through the small rectangular window on the second set of doors. No one seems to be around. She knocks on the heavy door, no response. She turns, sees a maintenance man at the elevator. The door of the elevator opens, the man steps inside, inserts a key into the panel.

"Wait," Lesa calls, strides across the floor.

The man straightens his arm, prevents the door from closing on her.

"I'm looking for—" Lesa stops, realizing how unreasonable she might sound. Fourteen hundred clients, one random maintenance man, what are the odds? Surely a hit and miss where Sylvie is concerned? The maintenance man holds the elevator door. Lesa reads the sign taped to the elevator: *Please do not encourage Melinda Carberry to use elevator unless supervised.*

"Going up?" he asks.

She smiles. How does he know she's not Melinda Carberry? Lesa tilts her head.

"Melinda doesn't read," he tells her.

"Who are you looking for?"

"Sylvie," says Lesa. "Burrows, Sylvie Burrows."

"You're close. She's one building over."

He points east.

"Second floor," he says, holding the door a moment longer than is necessary.

Lesa raises a questioning brow at him.

"Twenty-seven years," he explains. "Not many I don't know here."

She nods.

"Mind you'll have to take the stairs over there, those elevators won't go without a key."

He lets the door slide shut.

Lesa goes back outside, crosses the frozen grounds to the adjacent building. Same corridor, same hospital smell, same second set of locked doors. She goes through, commits herself, fully, completely. Sylvie is here, she can feel it, as if Sylvie's warm, moist breath is once again on Lesa's bare child-neck. Sylvie's stringy arms clung tight round Lesa's sturdy waist on the tricycle. Sylvie's heart racing in her chest, the thudding echo in Lesa's ear. Sylvie ready to bolt at any given moment, but Lesa, faster, always able to catch, calm Sylvie, rein in her aberrant impulses where her mother couldn't. Sylvie's unintentional guardian whether she wished it or not. The trepidation in Lesa's chest as she mounts the stairs swiftly two at a time, afraid that if she slows or, worse, stops, then she won't go any farther. So long away, so far ago.

The door at the top of the stairs shuts with a final metal click behind her, the same jarring mechanical click of her father's throat when he breathed in deliberately, deeply, as if preparing to dive beneath some watery surface while all of them, her mother, Nate,

Clare, Lesa, waited for him to surface once more, but he didn't. His still, quiet chest. Goosebumps on Lesa's skin then, now as she thinks about the ashen colour of her dead father's skin, his Sylvie-dark eyes wide open, blankness registering nothing/everything. The memory of him a heavy purple shadow on Lesa's soul, her grief returning again and again, seemingly indefatigable. Lesa shrugs the cold off her skin, sets her mind to present rivers.

The hallway is dim, dusklike. The overhead lights muted so she doesn't immediately notice the man lying on the floor as she stands in the corridor allowing her eyes to adjust to the semi-dark. She can see light from two doors at the end of the hall. When she does notice the small man curled at her feet, she starts. Lesa's heart thudding in her ears, she reaches behind, tries the door handle, locked. She looks down at the man. He's lying on his side, casual-like, as if on a Sunday picnic, his legs stretched out languidly, his hands busy with the peas-and-corn pattern of the stone floor. She notes the cauliflower ear, the serrated scar on his left brow, the mashed nose, the rough skin of a person who has spent too much time outdoors, the warp of his distorted face not unlike Sylvie's.

"Excuse me," she says, stepping cautiously over him.

He doesn't reply, doesn't move. His smooth fingers pulsing, pushing at the immovable light corn–dark pea pattern on the floor as if assembling a complex puzzle.

She walks down the dim corridor to the lit doorways. Peers into the wire-meshed window, sees a man swaying in the bright light of the day room like a sailor on an unsure ship. Another man, alarmingly large and primatelike, beats some unseen repeated path around the perimeter of the small room. Another still, clothed in nothing but a white towel wrapped loosely around his waist, sits with his naked back to her. Lesa doesn't pause at the door, knows the rooms are no longer co-ed as they were in the past but segregated now.

The women must be on the other side. She tries the knob on the other door, which is unlocked. She glances down the corridor, relieved to see the man still there, still ten metres out, the dark vacant corridor vaguely worrisome, though if push came to shove, she's sure she could defend herself. Regardless of the unlocked door, she knocks, a dull thud within. At first no one responds, then the short quick footsteps approaching. A caregiver, roughly the same age as Lesa's mother, looks out the caged window, unlocks the door from the inside, and pulls it open. She's dressed in a boisterous yellow smock plastered with happy faces.

"I'm sorry," Lesa says, "I wasn't sure if I could just come in."

The woman waves her hand to enter, retrieves her keys from the door.

The two of them stand in the doorway. Several women are in the room, none of them Sylvie. One, broad-shouldered like a swimmer, wanders around, talking to no one that Lesa can see. The woman's arms circling in time to Reba McEntire singing on the radio: *Oh, why is the last one to know, the first one to cry and the last to let go?* Lesa's eyes water, surprised at how close she is to letting go. She takes a deep breath to keep herself in check. The woman swims toward them.

"Watch the arms, please, Sherry," the caregiver says.

Sherry front-crawls back across the room.

"I'm not sure if I'm in the right place," Lesa says, spots another woman lying on a garish orange and brown flowered sofa, no doubt left over from the 1960s and kindly donated. The woman is watching *Murder, She Wrote*, soundless on a television housed in a huge wood cabinet also from the 1960s. This woman gets up swiftly and comes over to Lesa, stands uncomfortably close, examines the thick knit colours on Lesa's Alpaca sweater with her long, wizened fingers.

"You have a very nice sweater," she says crisply.

"Personal space, Barb," says the caregiver.

Barb doesn't flinch.

The caregiver eases her back a foot. Barb stands staring at Lesa as if waiting for some secret signal, a wink, a smile between them so that she might carry on with the Alpaca inspection.

"I've come to see Sylvie Burrows," Lesa says, avoiding Barb's intense face.

Barb steps forward.

"I would like to see that sweater again," says Barb.

"Not now, Barb. Come, let's talk out here." The caregiver moves out into the muted hallway, shuts the door so that Barb is forced instead to peer out the small rectangular window.

"And you are?" asks the caregiver.

"Her sister," Lesa says.

The caregiver extends a peach-flesh hand. Lesa shakes it, tries to release, but the caregiver hangs on, pumps her hand eagerly.

"How great! Sylvie will be so excited. She's having her morning bath at the moment. Can you wait? Are you in town for a while? Are you the older sister or the younger? How is your mother? We heard your poor father died. He came like clockwork once a month for ten years, and then suddenly, nothing. We miss him. Sylvie misses him. She likes men, doesn't get to see too many regular ones up here, although she had no idea he was her father, any more than she'll know you're her sister, but she'll be glad to see you all the same. She enjoyed your father's company, having tea and cookies, walking the grounds, especially when he pushed her on the swings. She loved that."

Seeing the dazed look on Lesa's face the caregiver stops.

I'm sorry," she says.

"No, it's fine," says Lesa, her head swimming with questions, no forthcoming answers. He came like clockwork once a month? His entire last decade?

Lesa hadn't known. She doubts her mother knew. Why hadn't he told them? Although if Lesa digs deeper to Wednesdays past she knows why: he came for the sake of her mother, his Sylvie, himself.

"I'm Marge Mabley." Still holding Lesa's hand, Marge pats it like a long-forgotten aunt.

Lesa clears her confused head.

"I'm Lesa, the older one. My mother is fine, and yes, I can wait, I'm sorry to have not called, I didn't know I was coming."

"No trouble there, why don't you come inside and I'll round up some tea and digestive biscuits. Do you like those? Or Peak Freans, maybe there's some leftover in the kitchen, I'll check with Cook. It's almost lunch; perhaps you'd like to join the ladies in the dining room? We only have eight ladies now, used to be we had a full house way back when, some thirty-two women, four to a room. What a circus that was! But we've expanded. Come I'll show you Sylvie's room. We've recently decorated, purple is her favourite colour, with rainforest, animals, parrots, you'll see. Sylvie loves it, spends a good portion of her day there. Oh, she'll be so happy you're here! They

156

don't get many visitors. Either the family lives too far away, or the parents are long deceased with our population here aging themselves, or the memory is too painful, better left scabbed over and forgotten. What did you say your name was again?"

Lesa draws a breath, can't think for the flash flood of Marge's words. Guilt slips across her tired face like a noticeable cloud.

"Lesa," she says, adding softly, "Lesa Burrows."

"Not married?" Marge Mabley asks, searching her peach-plump body for something: a jangle of metal. Lesa looks down at the ring of keys attached to the loop of Marge's purple cotton pants. And there also, below Marge, next to her soft white-soled nurse's shoes is the small man from the other end of the corridor. Lesa doesn't know how he managed to sneak up on them, slipping, sliding, possibly skimming the smooth surface of the cool granite floor. Not so much a whisper of his clothing or the deep, even breathing she can hear now coming from him, like that of a loyal, slumbering dog. Her body relaxes suddenly with the simple in/out of his measured breath. She feels extraordinarily calm in this moment, not guilt, nor alarm, hardly startled by this small man lying coyly on his side, his long legs thrust out as if posing for *Playgirl*. He extends his hand up to Lesa. And though Lesa doesn't understand the significance of it, she knows it's important that she take his flat, smooth-knuckled hand in hers.

"A regular Burt Reynolds, aren't we, Jimmy?" Marge laughs.

Marge reaches down, ruffles the man's thick tousled hair.

"Come, Sylvie awaits you."

Marge pushes the door, has to instruct Barb to back, back, back up another foot so she can get the door open.

"We have a lunch guest, Sylvie's sister."

Barb's face lights as does the woman's on the orange sofa.

Lesa hesitates a moment, holds the man's hand, waits instead for him to release her, not the other way around. When he does, he gazes up at her in the dim corridor, his grin entirely grateful.

Wednesday, July 1961 » Jacqueline, age 27

Jacqueline moves purposefully through the darkened house gathering toys, wiping the peanut butter from the walls, cupboards, off the kitchen table. She's in charge; this is her ball game, her baby, her first and last act. She's the driver now, no longer the passive passenger in someone else's car. She considers checking Nate and Lesa once more. But then—no. What would be the point?

Out of habit she goes down the hall, checks them anyway. They are both asleep on top of their covers. The house is sweltering with the closed windows, locked doors, impending storm. She stands a moment in the doorway looking at the back of Lesa's dishevelled strawberry-coloured hair, Nate's tan limbs splayed in every direction like an octopus. She could stand here all night, but she knows what she needs to do.

Jacqueline tiptoes into the living room to gather peanut-buttered-covered Sylvie from the chesterfield, carry her surprisingly lightweight, heavy-soiled body through the darkened house, past the hi-fi. No Ted Daffan singing the tragic anthem to someone's life, hers possibly. It doesn't matter now, all that matters is that Lesa and Nate don't wake, don't interrupt her action. She glides silently through the dining room, catches her reflection in the dining room window. She's light, transparent like a ghost, a wingless angel, a merciful God perhaps. She doesn't stop to choose.

Furtive, she makes her way through the kitchen to their garage. Pushes the door open with her back, is greeted by the heat, the humidity, the rumble of thunder in the distance, the mounting trace of exhaust in the closed garage, the mechanical growl of her husband's Plymouth Fury. She glances down at Sylvie in her arms. She's breathing deeply, evenly, the sleep of the dead, Jacqueline thinks. Sylvie always slept that way, even as a baby.

Jacqueline shifts Sylvie to her left arm so that she can open the door of the Plymouth with her right. She pulls the car door open wide, the smell of car exhaust assaults her nostrils, mixed in with the carbon monoxide that she can't see, smell. Odourless, invisible, the silent killer, killer of silence—all Jacqueline wants. Silence as measured against the endless, difficult matter of uncertain children, absent husbands, sketchy fetuses—her future led out in a kind of living hell. The silence of killers, her, Jacqueline. She holds her breath momentarily, then inhales deeply, decisively, welcomes the cloudy stupor of monoxide into her lungs as she does that first lingering cigarette in the morning, only this more effective, faster.

She slides into the vinyl seat with Sylvie in her arms and quietly clicks the driver door shut.

Wednesday, February 1973 » Lloyd, age 40

Corporal Lloyd skirts around the province's capital, not wanting to stop, wanting to make up for time lost, perhaps never found. But more than that Jimmy is calm in the back seat of the Camaro Z28 wolfing down the burger, both his and Lloyd's fries, the hot chocolate with the mile-high whipped cream. And, of course, the aftermath of the whole Burger Baron bedlam scene that neither one mentions. Lloyd thanks his lucky stars, the double V of his corporal insignias, that no one called in extra police to assist or Lloyd would have some complicated explaining to do.

After the burgers, Jimmy needs to go to the washroom. Lloyd bypasses the brief strip of gas stations, opting instead for the wide-open prairies and the cold shoulder. He pulls the car over and stops on the side of the road. Jimmy scrambles out of the back seat, clutching his groin like the child he is. Lloyd keeps his eye on Jimmy, not wanting to leave anything to chance. Jimmy may have a whole bag of tricks yet to revile the trusting public with. Corporal Lloyd surveys the white void of the February prairie. Something comforting in that, a blank slate, a clean bill in which to begin again, each day fresh, anew. Although this

Wednesday feels like the Twilight Zone, time without end.

He lights the remnants of his cigar butt in the ashtray, watches Jimmy relieve himself. A yellow streaming spray arced into the lightless day along the desolate highway to Red Deer. How long since he was last at Michener? When Sylvie was admitted, Lloyd calculates. Fall 1961. Though he's has never been inside Michener himself, can barely stand the thought of Sylvie's skewed features, so sweet, so flawed, so unfair—let alone set foot into an entire world full of God's imperfections.

Even then, when they admitted Sylvie in 1961, Jacqueline and Lesa did that. His wife and young Lesa walking hand in hand with small, buoyant Sylvie skipping along in the middle, like she was simply off to playschool. While Lloyd remained outside the low brick building with Nate and brand-new baby Clare. The three of them crouched beneath the barred windows in the heatless sun, the autumn air cool around them. Lloyd's breath in short gasps, his dark eyes wet beneath his impenetrable sunglasses.

Like offering your child up to strangers. Driving her out to the middle of a deserted field and leaving her there, Lloyd thinks, surveying the bleak prairies. But that wasn't the case for Sylvie. Sylvie required the special care, the medical expertise, a safe place, although no amount of rationale fully convinces Lloyd.

He feels his intestines shift, not from the burger or the black coffee but something else. He can do this, for the love of God; he's a grown man, a corporal in charge of a detachment, six constables beneath him, an entire town in his care, a wife, three, no four children, if he counts Sylvie. And Sylvie does count, thinks Lloyd, despite the unease he feels inside whenever he thinks of her, like an unfastened latch, a loose door in a windstorm. At the very least he can do this for Jimmy. If not for Sylvie, always Sylvie, in all ways his Sylvie away at Michener, but ever-present in his mind.

Jimmy opens the passenger door, climbs into the back seat. His stomach filled, bodily functions gratified. He curls onto his side, falls immediately into deep oceanic sleep.

Lloyd glances at his watch, shortly past three, just over an hour to Red Deer. He rolls the window down a crack to clear the glutinous haze of fatigue from his head. He needs to keep himself alert, get there before administration closes. He pulls onto the highway shortcutting through Beaumont, then onto Highway 2. Leduc on the left, Wetaskiwin farther east, and later the sign for Red Deer. The nearer he gets to Michener the more the disquiet rises in his intestines, the low pulsing of the live wire increasing beneath his shallow skin. Michener is the test, and Sylvie his last act.

Wednesday, October 1987 » Lesa, age 31

Lesa's lunchmates at Michener consist of Sherry the swimmer, personal-space-issues Barb, and a tiny woman in a wheelchair at the end of the wood table whose lunch will be consumed through a large red straw.

"A selective mute," says Marge Mobley.

"Selective?" Lesa asks. She's not heard that term before.

"She can talk, but she chooses not to."

Marge makes wide eyes at the tiny woman in the wheelchair as if to incite conversation. The woman returns her gaze evenly, calmly, mute.

Not seated yet is Rosalind, newcomer to the brightly lit dining room, who judders around like a caught dragonfly at a window. Rosalind comes with her own bottle of rosewater hand lotion that she carries from day break to day gone until she collapses in a worried heap onto her rose-coloured bed in her pinkened room across the hall from Sylvie's purple rainforest room.

"Everything coming up roses," Marge says in reference to Rosalind.

"Until age twelve she was perfectly normal, a promising pianist, a child prodigy. You should hear her play. Isn't that right, Rosie?"

Rosalind, intent on the lotion, ignores Marge, displays the pink-coloured bottle in her hands like a professional demo woman at the mall.

"May I interest you in some rosewater?" she asks Lesa.

Lesa looks across the table at Marge. Marge shakes her head, advises against it.

"No, thank you," says Lesa.

"Then she got hydrocephalus, that's water on the brain, you know, and she's been with us ever since. Has no memory of anything before that, her childhood, her heartbroken parents, everything gone, except for the piano, and now, of course, the lotion. No one knows where that came from."

Rosalind squirts a small knoll of pale lotion out onto her palm, smoothes it on her forearms.

"May I interest you in some rosewater?" she asks, sitting down next to Lesa.

"No, thank you," Lesa says, looking to Marge.

"Short-term memory loss." Marge tries to distract Rosalind by miming piano keys on her rose-softened arm. Rosalind pulls a dour face. She wants to interest someone in her lotion.

"Rosie, why don't you play something for us on the piano?"

Rosalind gets up off her chair with a force, stomps out. Then the piano starts up in the other room, and so do Sherry's circling arms. Lesa hazards a glance over at Barb across the table, who's been watching her the whole time. Barb's face nervous, intent, twitching with anticipation, waiting, it seems, for Rosalind to exit. She rises from her chair.

"Have a sit, Barb, lunch will be here soon," says Marge, without missing a beat. The caregiver so conditioned, so accustomed with the everyday happenings of the place, she needn't even glance over at Barb to know what's going on.

Barb shrinks back down into her chair, her keen face deflated.

"I have a dog," Barb says suddenly to Lesa, her voice clipped, sharp.

"What kind of dog?" asks Lesa.

Barb doesn't answer.

"What color is your dog?" Lesa tries again.

"White and black and some white."

Lesa smiles at the syntax of that.

"Big or little?"

No response, Barb's eyes a blank stare.

Then: "I have some super news to tell you," Barb says commandingly, an odd smile on her lips.

Lesa leans forward.

"I'm having a seizure right now."

"Is that a good thing?" Lesa asks, confused by the smile.

"No that's a bad thing."

Barb is silent, stares off into the kitchen.

After a moment she returns to herself: "What is for lunch?"

"Smells like meatloaf," Marge says. "Hold your horses, it'll be ready shortly."

Barb goes back to monitoring the kitchen.

Sylvie enters with a whoosh of freshly bathed scents, lavender, eucalyptus. Her black hair blow-dried and shining as if she knew today was the Wednesday Lesa was coming. Lesa stands up as Sylvie rushes the table.

"That purple lady give Sylvie some lunch?" Sylvie pointing her outstretched finger at Marge.

"That purple lady wants you to meet your sister," says Marge.

Lesa smiles expectantly at Sylvie. It does feels as if she's *meeting* Sylvie for the first time since they were both children.

"Sylvie's a sweet soul," Marge says, smoothing her hand across Sylvie's back. "I worked with her when she first came to Michener, on Ash Villa."

Lesa recalls her father driving past the forest area in between. Past the wood villas on the south side of Michener named for the trees: Juniper, Birch, Elder, Ash, Tamarack, Pine and Spruce. Her father driving their Plymouth Fury slowly, slowly as if to stall, as if he didn't want to reach their final destination. Ash Villa where Sylvie would live. Where her father would wait outside in the car. Lesa can't shake the jumble of trees and villas, childhood memories fresh in her mind. Instead envisions limbs and trunks and branches twisted up, wild, messy like the magpie nests of her youth—akin also to the crowded, moving mass of bodies in the day room when they came to see Sylvie as a child—like a kinetic, forsaken forest vying for space, for place, for illumination.

"Now, of course, Sylvie's on the north side with us," Marge says, tucking a black strand of stray hair behind Sylvie's elfin ear.

Sylvie pauses, looks bewildered. Some long ago remembered recognition? Lesa hopes. But no, Sylvie goes back to poking the air with her busy finger, her skin steamy, rose-coloured like Rosalind's wares. Then she makes her way to the end of the table next to the selective mute in the wheelchair. Lesa watches Sylvie; in fact, she can't take her eyes off her largely forsaken sister.

"And I told that girl she had red socks and my yellow shirt," Sylvie says, directing Lesa's caught eyes to her ill-fitting salmon sweatshirt and too-large black pants.

Then Sylvie opens her mouth and hauls out the set of pink plastic gums and white porcelain teeth to reveal the dark cavern inside. A backward wince, Lesa remembers when her father took Sylvie away, pre-Michener. Then for days after everywhere Sylvie went in their house the smell of burnt toast followed her.

"She had to have all her teeth removed, her gums cauterized because of the drugs," Lesa's mother explained at the time. Head down, her mother braided her fingers across her forehead and smoked one Peter Jackson after another in the grim silence of their living room.

Lesa imagines the residual smell of burnt toast lingering in the air above them, not only Sylvie's past, but her boyfriend's current burnt toast exhibit on Granville Island. The significance not entirely lost on her, although the status of her relationship with him remains adrift.

Sylvie waves the dentures over her head until Marge says she can set them on the table if she doesn't want to wear them right this moment. Sylvie lays the teeth down, strokes them ever so lightly with one finger like a small mouse, a pet hamster. Her dark, glittery eyes so like their father's, it makes Lesa's blood quicken through her body.

Sylvie sits down unceremoniously at the other end of the table.

Lesa's expectant face like Barb's deflated.

"Sylvie, come give your sister a hug!" Marge says.

Sylvie looks around, finds Lesa's strange face in the familiar room.

She gets up, unsteadily, lurches over, and rests her head briefly on Lesa's chest. Lesa puts her arm around Sylvie, which Sylvie thrusts off with considerable strength.

"Yeah you give that Sylvie some lunch now?"

Marge laughs. Lesa wants to cry.

"Yes, Sylvie, lunch is here," answers a woman in a long white apron, coming into the room with a low silver dining cart. Her skeletal shoulders bent as if from constant service even when she straightens them to remove the beige plastic lids. She sets down plates of steamed meatloaf and mashed potatoes and gravy, limp tossed salad, see-through plastic cups of fruit punch in front of each client. The woman singing their names half loud, mezzo forte, a cooking–singing prodigy like Rosalind playing the piano expertly in the other room. For the mute in the wheelchair, the bent cook slides the entire plate, salad, punch, and all into a blender, purees it, then pours the swampy brown liquid into a metal cup with a red straw. Sylvie makes for her chair.

"Milkshake à la meatloaf for Ms. Mira," the woman belts out, fortissimo.

"She's not deaf," Marge informs her.

The aproned cook winks at Lesa.

Lesa stands at the empty chair next to Sylvie.

"Mind if I sit here?" Lesa asks.

"Yeah okay that girl sit here." Sylvie jabs the meaty air with her pronged fork.

"Mind the weapon, Sylvie," Marge says.

Sylvie considers Marge for a moment, then lowers her fork submissively to eat her instant mashed potatoes and gravy. Lesa sits down, nauseated by the smell, the blendered food, stunned by the sight of Sylvie after all these years. Speaking Sylvie. Sparkling Sylvie. Grown Sylvie. No longer the frenetic, high-wire child Lesa recalls so vividly, the wild, impulsive, sometimes impossible sister. But here now a woman, not a year and some younger than Lesa herself. The same height, but slimmer through the hips, Sylvie's cheekbones finer, the backs of her delicate hands picked over in a self-obsessive layer of red scars that makes Lesa feel dark, cavernous, achy inside. Sylvie's slick, shiny, short-cropped black hair like a consolation prize.

Lesa watches Sylvie work systematically through the mashed potatoes, finishing them wholly before she begins on the salad. Obvious that she's saving the best for last, the steamed meatloaf. Lesa's head down, she can't eat, can't look at the selective mute in the wheelchair sucking tossed salad through a straw. Or Barb across the table watching her with all the desperation of a struggling swimmer, drowning perhaps in her trapped silence, Lesa can't tell. Or Sherry, the true swimmer, one hand still circling in the tainted air in harmony to Rosalind's *Ode to Joy*, the pace cheerful, fast, allegro. Pitch-perfect, yet so out of tune with how Lesa feels at this moment. Marge Mabley talking brightly, surreally to the apron-clad cook, both of them oblivious it seems to the despondent, trapped sorrow around her.

And Sylvie sitting next to her after so long, so many missed years. Her sister's freshly bathed flesh warm, welcome; Lesa's head down, tears drip into her mashed potatoes, the coagulated gravy.

Marge reaches over, lays her hand gently on Lesa's back. Lesa covers her face with her hands. Rosalind's *Joy* from the other room, in spite of her hydrocephalus, her short-term memory, her lost parents/leftover life, the music rising, surging. Rosalind's rosewater fingers building crescendo after crescendo on the ivory white keys, some black. Then the music stops—the silence in the dining room is raw, palpable. Lesa takes a ragged breath, feels her blood slow, hears the even cadence of her heart in the unexpected stillness.

When she is able, Lesa raises her head. So weary of guilt, remorse, of not being able to change things, she observes with fresh eyes. What does she see? She sees Sylvie's toothless gums, her hollowed cheeks. The small, quiet, pointed movements of her scarred hands accompanying the soft constant chatter, the innocent gaze across her sister's mature face intact, whole, despite that laden Wednesday so long ago in her mother's arms, her father's car, rigid in Lesa's mind. Despite her sister's life away from them at Michener.

She surveys the other women around the table. Neither helpless, nor the haphazard children at Michener, they, like Sylvie, are all grown up and hiding out in their adult bodies, concealed beneath wrinkled skin, failing flesh, falling hair, removable teeth. Living, breathing, growing older like everyone else—like Lesa, her mother. She glances at Barb, whose emotions shift across her face like clouds, a moving, visible mist. Sherry's unrestrained delight when Rosalind starts up again from the other room. This time softly, gently, pianissimo, a song Lesa doesn't recognize but is thankful for. Ms. Mira placid and selective in her speech, her wheelchair. Sylvie's dark eyes like a child's.

Lesa sees it now, couldn't before. *Theirs* holds a hidden prize. God's iconic/ironic gift: the child remains within. Ever-present and, with luck, Lesa hopes, inextinguishable.

The room fills again with noise, action: Marge goes back to her conversation. Barb wonders out loud what's for dessert. Ms. Mira sucks, Sherry swims, Sylvie eats her prized meatloaf. Rosalind finishes playing the piano, flutters back into the room with her bottle of rosewater.

Before Rosalind can ask, Lesa extends her hands.

"Yes, thank you, I need that now."

Rosalind's fervent smile as Lesa accepts a squirt on each palm, rubs the pink lotion in humbly, gratefully in the midst of Sylvie, in the company of fine women.

Wednesday, July 1961 » Jacqueline, age 27

For a brief moment Jacqueline must have dozed off, nodded and bobbed in the exhaust of a long, hot troubled day, jerked back into *being there* by the weight of her heavy head sliding down the warm glass of the driver's window. She feels the weight of Sylvie shift from her arms. The almost imperceptible swelling of baby in her thickening belly. She shakes her head; woozy, dizzy, weedy as the weak light seeping through the open garage door that she'd thought she'd shut. She squints sideways, and sees that, indeed, on her own volition, Sylvie has removed herself and instead slid down in the passenger seat next to her like a tourist along for the ride, a holidayer-in-arms ready for the road trip ahead, come what may. Jacqueline looks at Sylvie's small, thin face, brown from the sun, the jagged line dissecting her otherwise pink-child lips, the clumps of peanut butter in her normally seal-black hair. Sylvie's eyes closed, her body sticky with the close summer heat, the heat of the closed car.

Are you all right? Jacqueline asks, doesn't know if she's said it out loud or only thought it.

Can we do this? is what she really means.

Jacqueline strokes Sylvie's hard-sleeping face. Her own face in the rear-view mirror is strangely soft in the void of the thick, flat exhaust she can taste in the back of her throat. The monoxide tiptoeing into the car, her lungs like some distant clouds gathering on the horizon. Nothing to do with her, her Sylvie, her unborn baby. She glances at the light from the garage door, sees a muddled figure. She turns and waves. The figure doesn't wave back. Oh well, she thinks through the murk in her mind. So far removed, Jacqueline doesn't pay it any further thought.

She turns her attention back to Sylvie's face. So sweet, so simple, so utterly *trusting*. This last thought causing black thunderheads in the otherwise white stratosphere of her brain to seep, leach white over everything, like colourless candy floss in a white parade. Those high, puffy clouds where angels loll and God exists, perhaps even listens—like carbon monoxide. The black of her mind dissipates into the larger white before Jacqueline can retrieve it. Wait, she thinks, don't leave. But as swift as the objection came, it's gone.

Perhaps she'll just rest her eyes a minute; she's so damn lousy-drowsy. Her eyes are burning; she can hardly keep them open. She leans her head on the driver's window despite the perplexing figure that is now in motion moving around the side of the Plymouth Fury in slow time, not real. The figure's actions measured, deliberate. Jacqueline can't make out who it is. Her head is pounding from the colourless monoxide and she can't stop coughing, choking on the card exhaust. She tries to breath shallowly through her nose to quell the cough, she doesn't want to wake Sylvie.

In the distance Jacqueline hears the *tug tug* of the metal door handle, locked on her side. She shakes her head, tries to keep her eyes open, make out the figure at her door. Her head rolls wildly; all she wants to do is sleep, certainly that's easy. Not too much to ask for, is it? God knows she deserves it. She peers down at Sylvie, who is well on her way, her face already at peace. Her peaceful, trusting face. Wait, wait, Jacqueline thinks, recalling a vague idea, a black mark hanging in the whitened air before her smouldering eyes, palpable, visible so she thinks she can reach out and touch it. She tries, but it eludes her, disperses white again. But every time she opens her eyes, it's right there in front of her, why can't she touch it? She can see it as plain as Wednesday.

She struggles with the lassitude of her laden body, calls back the levitation games she played in her teen years: your body is heavy, your arms and legs like water-saturated logs, you're dead, you're dead, your head like—what? She can't remember. Her limbs *are* like logs, her body *is* seriously heavy, but her head oddly light as if someone is trying to force her back down into oblivion.

She hears Sylvie's door open, feels the whisper of not-so-thick air mixing with the monoxide. Someone far away is coughing. Who? She can't turn sideways; rather she rests her loglike limbs against the vinyl seats. The coughing persists, although hers has stopped, must be smoking all the livelong day that has quelled hers. Sylvie hasn't coughed once. With great effort she lifts one arm and drapes it across Sylvie's shoulders. She can feel Sylvie's small hands clutching her arm, pulling, pulling so that Jacqueline opens her eyes briefly and glances down at Sylvie, who for all intents and purposes seems fast asleep. She must need to go pee, Jacqueline thinks. Sylvie does that sometimes, rousts Jacqueline from her never-deep sleep to take her down the darkened hall to the bathroom.

Weary as she is, Jacqueline goes through the required motions in her mind. She pushes against the locked door and then rests from the exertion. Opens her eyes again to see that irritating black mark hanging in the air. She needs to get rid of that. She paws at it, it won't go away. Someone is in between her and Sylvie, moving, pushing Sylvie's silent body across the vinyl seats. Jacqueline hears the thunder outside fracture and split, the *plink plink plink* of rain, quickening, then pummelling down on the garage roof so hard that Jacqueline can scarcely breath amid the metallic roar. Heavy in herself, she glances over at Sylvie, instead sees a confusion of strawberry hair—vaguely familiar. She smiles lethargically, listens to the throbbing rain.

Then the tugging again. All right, Jacqueline thinks. Mother of mission, force of habit: get up, get moving, that's all she has to do. She's forgotten why they were in the car in the first place. Were they going somewhere? She doesn't drive. Something about the ball game, a play, someone's first act? She doesn't recall, but Sylvie needs to go to the washroom and if they don't do it now, there will be a much bigger mess to deal with after. Despite the miasma coalescing in her head, she unlocks the door. Oh yes; she needs to turn the engine off. She clicks the ignition, pushes the driver's door wide, watches as the interior cloud of car exhaust diffuses visibly, then vanishes into the larger air like magician smoke.

One leg out, then the other. Jacqueline rests another moment. Sylvie yanking her arm: Let's go, Mom, let's go, she says. Jacqueline doesn't pause to consider that Sylvie rarely speaks directly to anyone, let alone calls her Mom. She rises, her legs shaky, her mind a twirl like the Ferris wheel, like the Strawberry Swirl she took Sylvie and Lesa and Nate on last summer at the exhibition grounds, like—she loses her train of thought, feels Sylvie's tight grip on her hand, guiding, leading, pulling Jacqueline out of the car, the garage. Outside: the close heat, the unbearable humidity, a long hot troubled day. In its place, the rain pounding, the deep night air pulsing into her lungs breathable, bearable. Jacqueline inhales deeply, gives into her buckling knees, drops down to the wet grass, lies on her back. Feels the damp soak through her husband's sweatshirt to her freckled skin: cool, welcome. She can smell his scent again: musky, ambiguous. Regardless she misses him.

On her left, peanut-butter-slathered Sylvie is alert, awake, her black eyes glittering in the dark. On her right she just now realizes is Lesa. Lesa squeezes her hand, won't let go. The three of them lie on the soaked grass in the hammering rain, heavy limbs akimbo, their backs pressed firmly to the ground.

The rain lessens, the rudderless sky goes pitch-black, lucid, gradually clearing. They recline in the quiet aftermath. Sylvie chatters softly, points up at the first elusive stars that emerge, hardly yellow or discernable light, but *there* nonetheless; by her next-door neighbour's *God*, they are there. Though all she sees— when she looks over the narrows of her twenty-seven years—are people. The people she loves: her children, her husband, despite his shortcomings, the kind constable and his wife whose name she can never remember. Nary the ambiguous God. Only the godless imperfection of ordinary people. That she can manage, comprehend.

Jacqueline holds Lesa's hand, finds Sylvie's small, funny hands in the dark, squeezes them both, hangs on for bitter, dear, sweet life, like some shipwrecked sailor to hull. It's all she's got, everything she needs. She clings to her children, born, unborn, come what may, lets the tears run fiercely down her face.

This Wednesday passing like any other day of the week.

Wednesday, February 1973 » Lloyd, age 40

Coming into Red Deer on Gaetz Avenue, Lloyd's stomach is queasy from the greasy burger, the coffee, the prospect of Sylvie after all these years. His out-of-sight, out-of-mind method where Sylvie is concerned is no longer effective. The closer he gets to Michener Centre the more exacting is his mind. How many years since he laid eyes on his Sylvie? 1973 minus 1961. Twelve years. Beyond a decade now, well beyond the time when Jacqueline was pregnant with Clare, overwhelmed, despondent, alone, and adrift in the swirling mass, the Plymouth Fury, the man in the sage-coloured station wagon— the details of that day drilled into him by the constable from next door in his unspeakable absence. And where was he? Is he?

He doesn't even remember the name of the woman, like some God-abandoned rock star, like Keith Richards of the Rolling Stones, *what was your name again, luv?* Some woman he met some place, the both of them topped up with Crown Royal or vodka screwdrivers, or for him, the RCMP pile driver of the exhausting hours away from home. The things he's witnessed on the job that make him feel hopeless, a cart without wheels, make him believe the world *is* going to hell in a handbasket, coming to a Jehovah's

Witness end, the soldier going to war, nothing to live for, nothing to die for, except for the moment. The beautiful quixotic tangibility of a strange woman, the pervasive skin of the unknown, like alcohol, addiction itself. Nameless, anonymous, a shadowy place he can bury himself in.

No excuse, Lloyd knows, not then, not now. He glances in the mirror, his dark eyes tired, unreadable, incomprehensible even to himself, his wife. Lloyd knows Jacqueline is not obtuse; she has to have known all along. How could she not? Why she stays with him he doesn't know, but he's enormously grateful in this moment, this present pilgrimage to his cagey past. He bears the glut of his guilt, along with the weight of Sylvie behind him on his wheel-less cart.

Corporal Lloyd follows Gaetz over the bridge; the Red Deer River below frozen completely, nothing moves, nothing yields to the unforgiving Wednesday. Lloyd checks the rear-view mirror again, not for himself, but for Jimmy. It's been a good hour since he's heard a peep or whale blow from him. He doesn't see him. What the hell? No place to go, no stops along the way.

At the next red light Lloyd leans into the back seat, sees Jimmy Widman sleeping on the floor. His body curled round itself like a dog, the humped centre of Pete's Camaro is Jimmy's pillow. Must be what Jimmy's used to, doorways and alleys and floor mats, at least Michener has beds, warm, safe beds, a proper place to rest one's head.

Past the frozen river Lloyd accelerates up the hill, turns onto the road leading into Michener. The sprawling grounds are covered in snow. The low, flat brick buildings, north side, south side, the wooded area in between. He knows instinctively where the administration building is, that part of his exhausted brain suddenly alive, clear-thinking, purposeful as if his twelve-year absence was mere weeks, a month, lying dormant in quiet readiness for his to return to Michener, Sylvie, himself.

The administration building is tall, grand, red brick encasing a white stucco front spanning four storeys. He pulls up in front and stops, Pete's orange car idling pale exhaust in the stiff air.

"Stay put." He swivels around to see Jimmy on the floor.

Jimmy doesn't respond. Lloyd sits a moment considering his options, then decides his only option is to take the matter by the horn, Jimmy by the hand, and escort him inside. No sense taking chances at this point. He doesn't want Jimmy wandering the enormous grounds on his own, too cold out, and there's the forest-for-the-trees area he can't see beyond. He leans over, rouses Jimmy's shoulder. Jimmy looks up at him through his one good eye.

"Yes, ma'am," Jimmy says.

"Not your mother," says Lloyd.

"Yes, boss," says Jimmy, a rare moment of humour.

"Let's go on inside and see what we can come up with."

Lloyd shuts the ignition off, pushes his car door open. The cold air swings in, rouses the both of them. Jimmy exits the car like a dog, all fours on the frozen ground. Lloyd guides him gently to his feet, feels Jimmy's lightness lean into him. Together they walk the short flight of stairs into the grand entrance of the administration. The salt-and-pepper-haired woman at the front desk is on her feet before they even get through the double set of doors. She holds the door open, her face open, kindly, older than Lloyd by twenty years.

"Thank you," Lloyd says, leading Jimmy to a bench along the wall.

Jimmy slumps down; his fingers immediately busy tracing the grain of the wood. The woman gazes at Jimmy's worked-over face, the serrated line of stitches across his brow, the shut swollen eye, cauliflower ear. She mouths a voiceless *ouch* to Lloyd.

"He's all right, he'll be all right, if we can help him," Lloyd says.

"Nice ski suit," she says to Jimmy.

Jimmy grins without making eye contact.

The woman goes behind the desk, spreads her veiny hands across the mahogany top. The clock behind her reads 4:29. A full minute to spare.

"How can we help you?" she asks, speaking for herself, all of Michener.

Lloyd pulls the napkin out of his breast pocket, his flimsy excuse of a note, like an unofficial prescription from a dodgy doctor. He lays it on the desk in a crumpled mess, then he smoothes it out. She takes the napkin and reads it out loud.

"Michener Services: Please find Jimmy Widman intact, incompetent, and in need of psychiatric care. Sincerely, Judge Wade."

Corporal Lloyd watches her intently, the softened lines on her face, the delicate skin over her cheekbones slightly sunken, hollow. The strength of her jaw, the greying hair, the hilltop vantage of her settled years. Has probably seen everything from eternity and back. Inside, Lloyd's bowels are churning, the low live wire pulsing, increasing, charging through his every artery, pathway to his pumping heart. Lloyd hopes. He hopes for Jimmy, for Sylvie, himself even.

The kindly woman looks at him.

"Jonathan Wade, former lawyer?" she asks.

Lloyd nods; he'd forgotten Judge Wade practised mental health law in Red Deer prior to his appointment as a judge in Edmonton. Likely the reason why the judge chose Michener over Ponoka for Jimmy. Here the judge is a known, trusted quantity.

"Jimmy Widman?" She motions toward the bench where Jimmy was, is now curled on the floor, examining a real estate brochure someone has left behind.

"He's your man," Lloyd says.

She picks up the phone, waits while it rings rings rings, Lloyd can hear it in an office down the hall. No answer. The woman leans forward to gaze down the corridor. All the doors are shut; possibly everyone has vacated the premises. She looks at Lloyd. He drops his head to his chest. He can't look her in the eye in case she tells him there's nothing to be done today, tomorrow, perhaps? He can't wait, feels a sudden sense of urgency that he's not experienced before, a do-or-dire state of affairs. So used to pushing things down, so mired with the not-enough, seemingly never-enough of his work life, his personal life. He and Jacqueline unravelled, unravelling, his children he misses on a daily basis, might miss them forever if something doesn't give, doesn't change, doesn't *be* enough. This he knows today. He's sure of it. Jimmy's life depends on it. His too.

The woman dials another number on the phone, the ring echoes through the grand hall, bounces off the granite floor, the hollow high ceiling. She replaces the receiver, then flips through the Rolodex in front of her, tries again.

"North side, Dr. Maprin, please," she says.

Corporal Lloyd lets his breath out in a gush, hadn't realized he was holding it. He looks at Jimmy. Jimmy has meticulously shredded the brochure into a thousand tiny pieces in a neat pile on the peas-and-carrots granite floor. Now he's trying to fit the pieces back together. Could take a lifetime, Lloyd thinks.

Then the woman's up, buzzing and fussing about in the filing cabinet behind her, papers and forms in hand. She can't promise anything, it's not like you can simply walk into Michener and have someone admitted, especially an adult. Michener has had emergency admissions in the past, but always children and rarely at that. There's a process involved, you understand? Social workers, psychiatric assessments to be done by not one but three qualified doctors, although Doctor Maprin's the only one on today and he's on the north side, will be here shortly. Judge Jonathan Wade is no slouch, a good man, a fair man, that she knows, and clearly she can see Jimmy Widman is in need of some help, though that doesn't hold any water, won't necessarily get him admitted, and he, Lloyd, looks like he could use some help too, or perhaps just a solid night's sleep.

"Is he psychotic?" the woman asks, glancing up from her questionnaire form over at Jimmy.

Lloyd shakes his head. The woman ticks No on the box beside.

"A danger to himself?"

"He has his moments," says Lloyd, feels his pulse deadening.

"Suicidal?" she asks.

"No more than the rest of us."

"Yes or no?"

"Not in that sense."

She bypasses the box, goes onto the next question.

The woman holds Lloyd's gaze carefully for this last qualifying question:

"A danger to the public?"

The image of Jimmy standing the middle of the Burger Baron, his powder blue ski pants around his ankles, crying mothers, frightened children, disgusted men.

"Yes, he's a danger to the public," Lloyd says.

The woman nods, ticks off a corresponding series of squares on the form, raises her head.

"Enough?" Lloyd asks, can't even summon the strength to put it in a proper sentence—the weight of the day, his life in this simple question.

"Enough—for now," the woman answers.

Lloyd's shoulders drop. He smiles gratefully, helplessly at her.

Wednesday, October 1987 » Lesa, age 31

By the time she gets to her mother's car on the south side of Michener, the clock reads well past 2:00 PM. A three-hour lunch? She didn't notice the time go. Lesa's got to fly if she wants to make it back for dinner. She climbs in the Toyota, lights a much-needed John Player, flips the radio on, scrolls through the static until she finds a station. Country music—she leaves it on regardless. She pictures Sherry's arm swimming in rhythm to Dolly Parton as she drives down the hill, turns left onto Gaetz Avenue. The mid-afternoon traffic is light. She reaches Highway 2 in no time. Her mind on cruise control, she pushes the accelerator to the floor. Her mother's Toyota hesitates, the piston rods rattle in their cylinders at Lesa's sudden insistence but then settle into an even thrum in the fast lane.

No lingering thoughts of Sylvie. Sylvie is wholly unharmed, thriving even in her private child's life at Michener—Michener no longer the dire institution of Lesa's early memory. Lesa realizes only now, her parents' heart-rending decision to have Sylvie committed was not as black and white as she thought. Not simply a case of a difficult child, of a mother's Wednesday gone horribly awry. But full consideration given by her parents for all of them: Sylvie,

Nate, Clare, Lesa too. The water already under their bridges, a possible lifetime of bridges in need of constant repair, the reason matters not, what matters is that Lesa gets home in time for the monument of her mother's memorial dinner before she inflicts further damage.

She drives in the fast lane, passing a line of army trucks. The khaki-clad drivers honk and wave as she blurs past them before they turn off at Penhold. Then car after car after pickup truck until soon she's solo on the highway for as far as she can see on the wide-open prairies. She keeps her eyes alert for wayward coyotes. Olds, Didsbury, Carstairs; approaching Crossfield she scans the side of the road for her Superwoman boots, doesn't see them, hopes the waitress rather than the wilful October wind got them. She relaxes into the rhythm of the tires on the smooth asphalt, rips freely along hampered by nothing more than her want/need to see her mother.

On the outskirts of Calgary, past the line of available gasoline stations around Airdrie, two suburbs out from her mother's neighbourhood, her mother's car shrugs and stutters, refuses to accelerate. Lesa comes to a rolling stop on the shoulder, scans the dashboard for the emergency lights, sees the fuel gauge on empty. She hadn't noticed.

She climbs out of the car, the wind gusting, swirling grey road dust, carrying precious topsoil across the barren prairie. She retrieves her purse, her silver cigarette case from the front seat, the half-smoked joint inside that she considers seriously before flicking it off into the ditch below. Locks the car door, then she slides down on the passenger side of the car, shelter from the unceasing wind, pulls blue-suit man's vomit bag out of her purse. Folding the bag into a neat origami Air Canada airplane, she raises her hand up, allows the pulling wind to take it. She watches the paper plane lift and swoon for a moment, riding the extraordinary invisible waves, the plane swelling high, higher on the October air. Then the plane loses momentum, comes crashing down onto the stubbed remnants of last year's wheat.

Protected against her mother's car, Lesa smokes a cigarette in the tempest wind, weighs her gasless options. She could flag someone down. She could find a pay phone. She could call her brother, Nate.

She won't do any of those things.

A cluster fuck of God-given karma—Lesa knows it.

No more, no less. Reparation.

She stands up, begins the long walk toward her mother's house.

Wednesday, July 1961 » Jacqueline, age 27

Jacqueline wakes in the black of her own bed, can't immediately recall how she got there. But here she is in their marital bed, strangely fresh, alert at—she rolls over, squints at her Timex watch on the nightstand—3:35 AM. She reaches her arm instinctively across the double bed. No Lloyd. The house is deathly quiet; are her children sleeping?

Programmed, her body leads her down the dark hall first to Sylvie's room. She peers inside, sees Sylvie uncovered, coiled as she always sleeps at the foot of her single metal bed. Jacqueline tiptoes in, guides Sylvie gently up to the cool pillow, pulls a light sheet over her body curled like the fetus in Jacqueline's womb, like the circles Sylvie draws so flawlessly. She smoothes her hand over Sylvie's face, traces her finger lightly if only to soften, ease the jagged scar across Sylvie's pink lips. The nutty scent of peanut butter on Sylvie's skin. She checks Sylvie's arms and legs, mostly washed clean by the thunderstorm, although there are still clumps of peanut butter still in her black hair, the least of her concerns after this nightmare of a Wednesday.

She watches Sylvie's small chest breathe evenly, in and out, in and out, strong, smooth, involuntarily. There is a quiet strength in children that Jacqueline never noticed before, at least not consciously, not determined by straight or jagged, skewed or unskewed, but some *thing* intrinsic, innate, built-in. Beyond Sylvie, beyond Jacqueline even. Jacqueline can feel the metal burrs beneath her skin disband, disperse, released by the enormity of this simple understanding. So much so that she wants to roust Sylvie, pull her close, whisper in her faultless ear that she's lovely, she's wonderful, she's strong—a perfect girl in a defective world. Sylvie is everything she needs to be.

But Jacqueline doesn't want to wake Sylvie from the rare ease of her sleep. Instead she gets up, lingers another moment watching Sylvie from the doorway, then goes down the quiet hall.

In the other bedroom, Jacqueline finds Nate sprawled on his back, his toddler face flushed from the heat. Jacqueline slides the window open; the next day's air skims in cool, fresh, unsullied into her children's room. Lesa's asleep on the other bed, changed out of her wet skort and blouse into one of Jacqueline's T-shirts, far too large for Lesa's five-year-old body. Jacqueline leans close, pushes Lesa's strawberry hair off her freckled cheeks, tries to smooth out the perpetual rat's nest at the back of Lesa's head. She can't do it now, but come morning, Jacqueline knows that she owes, bare minimum, she owes Lesa a shampoo and a bubble bath. She keeps her hand on Lesa's sweltering back until she feels the heat release.

Then she gets up and wanders down to the living room. Startled to find Lloyd bowed and pressed against the hard curve of their red and black tartan chesterfield. She doesn't know when or how he got there without her hearing him. He's here, alive, still in uniform, flat asleep. She sits down beside him. His skin emits the stale scent of alcohol: warm, sweaty, musty. Does he smell of other women too?

She's not sure, just knows in some warped way that she needs him. No, he's not what she bargained for, not nearly as perfect as Sylvie's circles, but as time will inform her, things seldom are.

She watches the sharp line of his face, the same rise and fall of his chest, as Sylvie's, as her own. She lies down in the small, yielding space of him, slides back into the skin of herself too, also, for better or worse. She's in it for the long haul, she always has been.

Wednesday, February 1973 » Lloyd, age 40

Relieved of the weight of Jimmy Widman, Corporal Lloyd walks out into the cold air. He looks across the sprawling grounds of Michener, can see a teeter totter submerged in the snow. A metal slide coated in hoarfrost, the steep crystalline length of it, the white jagged edges. An empty swing set motionless in the dwindling light. He rolls his head side to side. He's tired, so goddamn weary-dreary, he'd like to curl up in a snowdrift and give into his fatigue. Relieved but not released. Not enough yet, but soon, sooner than he thinks.

If he could see through the jumbled scatter of poplar trees in between, past the naked winter forest in front of him, he'd be able to see the north side where Sylvie resides. The low, flat-topped brick buildings in strict rows, as if to bring order to the chaos within. The barred windows that make his chest seize, his throat knot. The live wire beneath his skin more alive then ever. He breathes consciously in and out, his breath tangible in the air. He can see it as clear as Wednesday. He zips up his RCMP parka, strides across the lot to the orange Camaro, gazes once more through the trees. He'll walk instead; the cutting air feels good on his face. In fact, he requires it.

The straight road that connects Michener south to Michener north has yet to be plowed. Lloyd follows the road, wades through the deep snow, glad for his knee-high Strathconas. His one gloved hand warm, the other he stuffs into his pocket, the car keys metal-cold to his touch. Beyond the forest, the frozen grounds stretch well off into the distance, farther than he can see. Territory he's not familiar with, some unknown ground he's not stood on. The muted light is growing grey over the horizon, darkening not only for dusk, but something else too? Snow perhaps, thinks Lloyd, pulls his parka closer around his body, the temperature dropping with the light. The weight of his leather boots, the heavy snow reaching his knees at points, the pending snow in the western sky.

His overwhelming fatigue as he traverses the wide-open space to the brick buildings, the precision of their rows reminding him of the row housing he and Jacqueline initially lived in. The row of houses adjoined, identical on the outside, though none housed anything inside like theirs: his uncontrollable, often inconsolable Sylvie, his island-stranded wife, who needed him then, not necessarily now, his children he missed, still misses.

He feels his body growing weak, though he's reached the broad sidewalks on the north side, which are shovelled clear, but still his body weak. He notices his ragged breath, edged like the hoarfrost on the metal slide. He spots a bench outside the first building, not Sylvie's, he knows. Her building is farther along, somewhere in the middle, not sure of the number, he knows it's across from a small canteen.

He sits down on the bench; the cold sneaks up beneath his pressed shirt, beneath his undershirt, under his skin, finds his core.

His arms, legs feel useless, exhaustion hitting him like a two-by-four, a brick wall he's run up against. He doesn't know if he can even stand at this moment, let alone stride through the maze of brick buildings in his stiff boots, find his Sylvie, look into her skewed face. He takes a shallow breath in the bitter air. Could it be the result of a long, difficult Wednesday? Why he's so tired, so weak? He doesn't know. Though he suspects it goes further, like the grounds he can't see past. Like his life past, his future, the road that lies ahead.

When enough is enough?

He tries to breathe more fully, revive his failing body, his struggling mind, but the cold air is useless to him. Lloyd looks up at the sky, the light almost gone now. The black seeping over, the few streetlamps along the sidewalk have blinkered on, throw a muted yellow on the frozen ground. Large white snowflakes are floating down from the dark sky. A group of caregivers in the distance, their voices growing louder as they approach, nine or eleven of them, Lloyd guesses. As they draw closer, he sees not all of them are caregivers, some are the clients they care for. He can tell by the peculiar gaits, the odd hunch of shoulders, the ill-fitting clothing, the herky-jerky motions of hands and bodies forever busy with their surroundings, their inner worlds, not aware of what's around them. He watches the group make their way to the building next door, the outside light of their two-storey brick home burning brighter than any streetlamp could.

The caregivers stop, mill about the lit entrance before going inside. Lloyd can see the burning red embers of the caregivers' cigarettes in the dark. Small talk, laughter from the caregivers, the patients themselves waiting, some wandering in circles, most content enough to be outside in the dark, in the falling snowflakes. One of them lies down in the snow drift piled high from the shovelled walks, the building light illuminates him or her. He can't tell. A small man? No, Lloyd thinks, not male, but female, a young girl, surely by the pink parka she's wearing. A male caregiver goes over, stands beside the girl on the ground.

"You all right down there?" the caregiver asks the girl.

She doesn't answer. The caregiver glances over at Lloyd on the bench.

"You all right?" he asks.

Too weary to make conversation, Lloyd nods.

"Business?" The caregiver spots the RCMP insignias on Lloyd's parka.

"In a matter, yes," Lloyd says.

The caregiver raises a brow.

"Good business," Lloyd reassures him.

The caregiver goes back to the business of the girl on the ground. She sticks her tongue out to catch the drifting flakes of snow. And without asking, without the caregiver saying her name, Lloyd knows. The visual clues: the glint of black hair in the yellow light, the skewed face, her pointer finger jabbing pointedly at the sky, the snow, the blue halo around the streetlamps, the sheer excitement of being out at night, likely. But even more, Lloyd *knows* by the tightening in his paternal chest, the live wire coursing fully through his body now, electrifying.

Of course it's Sylvie. His Sylvie, like a paradoxical gift from heaven, like the falling snow, the blackening night, his growing strength, his failing body—his fate folded up in his back pocket. He sits up, watches her intently. She's older by twelve years. Her teenage face the ghost of his four-year-old daughter, but present at his feet, alive, a shimmer in the cold light he's been missing: Sylvie, not four feet away, her arms and legs swimming X, making angels in the snow possibly for him?

Lloyd makes no move to get up, traverse those four crucial feet across the frozen ground. So close, so far, too much, too little his strength. He doesn't know if his trembling legs can bear the exhilaration, the tangibility of this beautiful moment. Everything he's lived for, everything he'll die for, here and now, present, accounted for, accountable. Almost enough.

Not now, he decides on this fleeting Wednesday. He'll be back— that he knows, so that he'll have something precious to hold on to.

Too little, too late? He doesn't think so.

He watches the snow float down from the black sky glinting like fallible stars when they catch the streetlamp. Sylvie sprawled on her back, arms and legs in constant motion, catching the yellow lights on her tongue.

The caregiver finishes his cigarette, crushes it out on the sidewalk beneath his rubber heel. He guides Sylvie gently to her feet, brushes the snow off her back, her pink parka.

"Let's get you inside, Ms. Sylvie," he says, nods at Lloyd.

Lloyd smiles in the dark. The live current coursing through him warms his weary core.

The caregivers round up the wandering patients, cajole, shepherd them kindly toward the low-slung brick buildings. Sylvie's soft, ceaseless chatter in the quiet dark. The straight line of her delicate shoulders as her caregiver soothes her, steers her toward the open door. Sylvie's dark mouth catching the snow one last time before she goes inside, looking back, laughing, pointing, waving, watching the man on the bench (him) while Corporal Lloyd watches her disappear down the long narrow corridor.

This picture he'll file away along with the living faces of all his children. Sylvie's shimmering hair, her face alight, excited, oblivious of who he is, but content enough he sees. He'll carry this image in his head like placing a photograph in an album that he can refer to later on, when he lies eleven years from now in a colourless hospital bed identifying his tinted past so acutely, so vividly, so bright, so dim, fast, slow—a silent private movie intended just for him. So that when he's finished, when his past catches up to his present moment, then he's done enough.

Corporal Lloyd stands up in the black night, the yellow light, the white falling snow melts on his face. He looks at his watch, thinks of Jacqueline's violet eyes in wait of him, he hopes. He's a man of some luck. He knows it now. If he hurries he can make it home before midnight, before he misses yet another Wednesday.

Wednesday, October 1987 » Lesa, age 31

She arrives late at her mother's house, well past dark, well past the time of her father's memorial, her mother's dinner. Doesn't bother ringing the bell or knocking, she knows the front door is unlocked, now that Sylvie no longer lives at home. Before she goes in, Lesa stands on her mother's front step gazing at the sky, no stars, no moon, no light. No lights on in the house either. Has her mother gone to bed?

She opens the screen door, pushes hard on the wood door that normally sticks, but releases easily this time with a silent *whoosh*. Her mother must have gotten it fixed since she was last home. Perhaps other things have changed over the course of her absence? A good thing? she wonders. *No that's a bad thing*, she hears Barb's pointed words in her head. She draws a sharp breath to steady her nervous stomach, takes her tennis shoes off, places them neatly aside the welcome mat. When she rises she sees the red burning ember of a cigarette in the dark of the living room. Not Nate, he doesn't smoke.

"Mom?" she asks but knows instinctively the breadth of her mother's smoking, the same measured pause and ensuing hesitant quiet when her mother calls long distance, smokes on the other end of the receiver. Lesa waits in the living room for her mother's inhale, the exhale, the quiet, but nothing comes after.

What can she say? How can she explain? She can't. She's here. Better late than never? Possibly better never? She doesn't know. Her mother is hesitant. Lesa traverses the lightless room she knows so well, takes a seat on the sofa across from her mother who sits in the familiar/familial green chair. The synthetic fabric of the chair looped in so many tiny razors that cleaved into their predisposed skin over the years like finely honed tools of torture. The same torturer's chair her father used to sit in late at night. The same chair her mother is sitting in now.

"Mom," Lesa says, wishing her mother wasn't in that chair.

Lesa hears her mother's uneven, ragged breath in the dark. Her mother doesn't answer. The darkness prevents Lesa from rising up, going across the carpet to her mother, throwing her arms about her, inhaling the strong scent of Chanel No. 5 her mother wore like a sheltering moat amid the rank of her father's cigars.

No rising, no arms tonight, no perfume that Lesa can discern, only the indiscernible silence, the dark room. Lesa watches her mother's inert cigarette, no doubt the ash growing long, the red glowing ember waning in the blackness in danger of burning out entirely.

Without permission Lesa reaches across the fake wood coffee table, turns on her mother's imitation Tiffany lamp. The light is minor, slight, without fortification. Lesa can't bring herself to look at her mother's face. Not yet. Looks instead at the dining room table. Her mother has gone to the trouble of using the white crocheted tablecloth Lesa's grandmother made, the matching stiff-starched swan in the centre holds the last remaining chrysanthemums from her mother's garden.

Her best silver, her Noritake China, the black and white picture of her father in his RCMP dress serge rests against the white swan. Two candles untouched, unlit. One place setting remains. Her mother has pulled out all the stops: dead fathers, departed grandmothers, declining flowers. Nate's likely gone back to Ottawa. Lesa's missed him, her mother's memorial dinner. The memory of her father lies in the room like fall frost. She wraps her arms about her body for warmth. She's sorry now, so sorry for those years of defiant rancour, her stubborn daughter doggedness, her mother's solitary grief, her father's regrets, the complicated matter of Sylvie.

What now? She doesn't know. Her fierce heart rises at the back of her throat. She knows not where to begin, but only to begin.

"Did you know he went to see Sylvie every month his last decade?" Lesa asks, looking for the first time in three years at her mother.

Her mother's lowered head, the grey strands dominant now over the normally red-hennaed hair. In the silence the forced air from the heat vents, the sudden catch of her mother's breath. She hadn't known either. Her mother raises her head. The black mascara from her eyes a moist charcoal river down her cheeks.

"Your hair," she says, breaking the awful silence.

Lesa reaches up, touches the blunt crop of her black-dyed hair. She'd forgotten.

"For Sylvie," Lesa says.

"I told Nate I thought you'd gone there," her mother says. The shiftless ambiguity of Lesa's day, not so much the risk in her mother's mind, only Lesa's. The realization that her mother knows her better than she does.

"Nate?" Lesa asks.

She's sorry to have missed him.

"He's gone out with friends," her mother says. "He'll be back."

Her mother lowers her head. Lesa can smell the burning filter of her cigarette.

"Sylvie?" her mother whispers.

"She's fine," says Lesa. "You'll see."

Tears well up again in her mother's lovely violet eyes. Her mother no longer hiding behind darkened sunglasses. Remorse so deep that her mother can't even think of Sylvie without going back to that Wednesday in July? Lesa can only guess, but it doesn't matter, what matters is the release. Lesa remains on the sofa, waits/wades in the depth of her mother's rivers.

Watching her mother across the room, Lesa gleans only now, only after Lesa's own dreadful Wednesday—that it wasn't any lack of love for Sylvie on her mother's part, but too much love: scared love, safe love, the sweet/despondent love only a mother can have.

Lesa crosses the carpet, takes her mother's duty-bound hands in hers, tries to wipe the river away from her mother's face, but once flowing, it doesn't stop.

"Did you love him, Mom?" Lesa scarcely whispers, afraid to say her father's name outright, afraid of what her mother might say. That long-remaindered embrace with the constable that lived next door to them in the row housing when Lesa was five, her mother essentially alone with three children, including high-wire Sylvie, baby Clare on the way, her father seldom home. Was their marriage sheer *need*, outright necessity, without choice—loveless? Did her mother stay despite herself for the sake her of children? Lesa doesn't want to know, but *needs* to know for the sake of the things she will carry forward from her mother's past—the sake of her own future.

"Yes," her mother says, as if she can read Lesa's interior mind.

"I didn't always like him, but I always loved your father. At the core your father was a good man."

The ash from her mother's expired cigarette drops to the hardwood floor. Neither of them bothers with it.

"Things have a way of evening out over time," her mother says softly.

Lesa wraps her mother in her arms like the child she doesn't have. The children she will one day hold in this limitless/faultless way that her mother has for all of them. Her children's father? Lesa hasn't thought about it until now. Neither blue, nor burnt toast, she decides, but more, much more.

When her mother quiets, Lesa releases her, goes into the large kitchen to retrieve a box of tissue. The stove light is on. She pulls open the warm oven, smells fried chicken, gravy. Not something Nate would have preferred, but Lesa's favourite. She lifts the glass lid on the casserole dish, pulls out a piece, picks the seasoned meat off the bone, and pops it into her mouth. Realizes how wholly empty she is after this day, feels her knees give into fatigue. She steadies herself against the Frigidaire in the dim light of the stove, the warmth of her mother's chicken in her belly. She eats slowly, purposefully, until the strength comes back into her. She shuts the oven door. On her way back into the living room she takes her Bic lighter out of her jean pocket and lights the candles on the dining room table.

Her mother is silent, spent, mascara stains down both cheeks.

"Come," Lesa says, taking her mother by the shoulders.

Her mother rises from the green torture chair. Lesa leads her past the dining room, into the small bathroom off the large kitchen, sits her down on the closed toilet seat, and opens the medicine cabinet. Fishing through her father's leftover medication that her mother can't bring herself to throw out, Lesa finds her mother's meagre bag of makeup. A single tube of red lipstick leftover from Lesa's childhood, she's sure, can recall the few times her mother wore it. A plastic case of red blush the colour of clown's cheeks, no eye shadow ever, a slim tube of clumpy black mascara. Lesa leaves the bathroom, comes back with two Johns and her own makeup bag.

"Let's start over," she says to her mother, who accepts the cigarette, lets Lesa light it after her own. Her mother inhales deeply, so does Lesa.

Lesa takes out her cleanser, gently wipes the mascara from her mother's face with a cotton ball. Up close Lesa sees the minute fissures of red blood vessels, a lifetime of them broken across her mother's freckled skin that Lesa never noticed before. Had they always been there? Lesa wipes harder, hoping they'll be magically erased, but she knows better. She looks into her mother's glassy eyes, digs out her purple eyeliner.

"Shut your eyes," she says.

Her mother does so, obediently. Lesa notes the creased lines running crossways on her mother's forehead, her unplucked eyebrows, her mother never one to take time for herself. Lesa cups her mother's soft aging face in her hands, the same way her mother used to in the bathtub, gently catching the small of Lesa's child head in her steady palm, likely also Sylvie's, Nate's, and Clare's, while she rinsed the shampoo out with the large plastic measuring cup. As if her mother could measure the love she felt for all of them each time she bathed them, washed their hair, clothed them, tucked them into bed each night.

Lesa looks at her mother's closed eyes, expects her mother might open them, some memory of this long-forgotten ritual, this practised remembrance between a mother and her children, but her mother doesn't open her eyes. Seems she's given in fully, let Lesa take the reins. In this moment, Lesa realizes her mother has had no one to take care of her, that she's raised her children, buried both her parents, nursed a dying husband, and now she's alone. Lesa has to steady her shaky hand to make the purple eyeliner skim over the surface of her mother's pale lids. Lesa traces her mother's uncomplaining, wordless mouth with raspberry lip pencil, follows the curved contour of her mother's still-full lips. Where her mother has had no keeper, Lesa is/will be.

Lesa flicks her cigarette into the chipped enamel sink that her mother has touched up temporarily with Wite-Out, examines her own face in the silver-flecked mirror. In the everyday light of her mother's bathroom, she sees the sliver of her mother, her father, Sylvie too, beneath her brown freckles, the water green of her eyes. Lesa pulls out her face powder, brushes it lightly, softly across the deficit of her mother's face, along her high cheekbones, over her strong jaw, and finally covers over the tiny red fissures beneath the surface of her mother's skin, if only to make them both feel better for the time being.

»»Acknowledgments

My thanks to the Michener Centre in Red Deer for their kind help given toward my research. In particular, Margaret Rumsey, who shared numerous working life stories of Michener, both present and past. Dr. Robert Lampard, for taking the time to answer my many, many questions. And thanks also to the security staff, who immediately questioned my driving, walking, skulking about the grounds, usually within minutes of my arrival. When I told them who I was and what I was doing, they graciously unlocked the no-longer-in-use buildings and allowed me to walk through, thus sparking both childhood memories along with the current-day surroundings of a wonderfully evolving Michener.

Special thanks to my sister, Jody Kvern, and the lovely ladies of West Terrace Three. Thanks, also, to the fine, long-standing women who care for the Terrace ladies.

My mother for not being the mother in the story, her many years of daughters, service, love, guidance through less than perfect times. Her continued years, love, guidance in our adult years. My father, whose bright presence I miss daily.

My thanks, yet again, to the gentle, funny, trusting, highly concise editing of Lee Shedden, and his wife, Fiona Foran, for her intuitive reading and thoughtful insights.

My thanks to Brindle & Glass Publishers, to Ruth Linka for her coastal support of prairie writers.

The Alberta Arts Foundation for their financial support in making *Sylvie* possible.

My constant sisters: Kelly Gray, Bobbie Charron, Dani Kvern.

My tall, great, growing-in-all-ways guys: my artist husband, Paul Rasporich, whose unvarying husband/artistic support allows me to write all the livelong day, my boys, Kai and Seth, who are ever-patient, always sympathetic. Writer/mothers are not the easiest to live with, and yet they do.

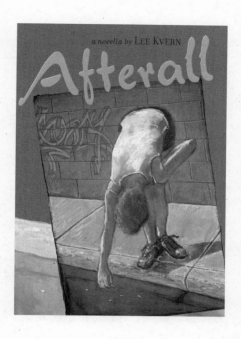

Afterall
by Lee Kvern
978-1-897142-01-1 • $19.95

One night after dinner, Beth impulsively announces that she's going to spend a night on Vancouver's streets in commiseration of the homeless. Unexpectedly, her friends' nine-year-old son Mason wants to go with her. Disaster, of course, ensues.

"The novella's saucy voice generates real narrative pull and neatly folds together high comedy and social satire."—*Vue Weekly*

Lee Kvern has a BFA in Visual Communications from the Alberta College of Art and Design. She has studied writing at the Humber School for Writers, the Banff Centre for the Arts and Athabasca University. Her short fiction has appeared in various literary magazines. She lives and writes in Alberta.